TRUE SON

SEVEN ARROWS

BALBOA.
PRESS

A DIVISION OF HAY HOUSE

ISBN: 978-1-4525-6036-6 (sc)
ISBN: 978-1-4525-6035-9 (e)

Balboa Press books may be ordered through booksellers or by contacting:
Balboa Press
A Division of Hay House
1663 Liberty Drive
Bloomington, IN 47403
www.balboapress.com
1-(877) 407-4847

Front & Back Cover Design by Don Knight
Art & Graphics by Thomas Coates
Editorial Review by Ted Meske
Native American Critiquing by Itswoot Wawa (Bear Who Talks Much) Chief Roy I. Rochton Wilson - Cowlitz Tribe

Because of the dynamic nature of the Internet, any web addresses or links contained in this book may have changed since publication and may no longer be valid. The views expressed in this work are solely those of the author and do not necessarily reflect the views of the publisher, and the publisher hereby disclaims any responsibility for them.

The author of this book does not dispense medical advice or prescribe the use of any technique as a form of treatment for physical, emotional, or medical problems without the advice of a physician, either directly or indirectly. The intent of the author is only to offer information of a general nature to help you in your quest for emotional and spiritual well-being. In the event you use any of the information in this book for yourself, which is your constitutional right, the author and the publisher assume no responsibility for your actions.

Printed in the United States of America

Balboa Press rev. date: 10/24/2012

Dedicated to the Truth that sets everyone free

Contents

Introduction

It was a very big surprise when I received the idea for this book. This huge idea came as a ball into which I could see all the main characters and the entire unfolding of the whole story which I knew was to be a novel--which in itself was a huge surprise. That the idea of the book came from Spirit deep within me, I could not argue, thus there were parameters within which this story could be told. There could be no embellishments or imaginary intrigues that could be incorporated into it. The story as it was received had to remain as I received it.

In a very simple way, this book is mankind's graduation story of its transitioning from these current times of great discord into the new cycle of Spirit's heavenly plan, a plan of spiritual Brotherhood that has been in the works for Ages.

Perhaps the reason that I was to be the author of this story was because in the Spring of 2011 I had a sudden shift in consciousness from being a part of this slowly crumbling civilization of western culture to that of being Native American in consciousness. It was a profound experience, as I realized that I was truly more in tune with the connectedness of everything that is an intrinsic part of the Native American ways. It was and still is beautiful to actually feel being a part of the wholeness of everything, something which the strong individualistic nature of our culture does not embody. Seemingly, today, everything on our planet is sacrificed for the sake of money, an unknown attitude in Native American culture.

Little did I know that when I experienced this beautiful, freeing shift in consciousness to actually feeling like I was much more Native American Indian than I had previously felt, I did not know there would come this responsible opportunity to write this novel. Thus I was able to write feeling-wise from the Indian that I am. In many ways I am still a part of this wrestling, trying-to-survive civilization, but do not feel that I am of that same type of energy.

There are enough novels that contain many of the insidiously harmful things that we do to one another, so there was no need in the mind of Spirit that anything of that nature had to be included which would detract from the spiritual, uplifting nature of this novel. It is my hope that you will identify with the good feelings that are sprinkled throughout these pages, and that you will gain an insight or two into your own divine nature.

Chapter 1

Deep Reflections

Joey was watching Winnie's face; her eyes closed and he felt her hand go limp in his. Winnie was exhausted after a long night of waiting to deliver. She had been given two pills--one to relax her and one to let her sleep. Without her having had any contractions for the last three hours or so, the waiting all night had been hard on both of them. Dr. Ross had suggested that the pills might relieve the tensions, but he too was at a loss why the contractions had stopped.

Joey eased his hand out of Winnie's thinking that he might get a couple of winks. He relieved himself and went into the little waiting area for expectant fathers. He sat down and closed his eyes, but his mind was racing. For the first time the thought crossed his mind about the possibility of losing Winnie through childbirth. He had heard of such incidents. That shook all possibilities of sleep from happening because of the long number of fearful thoughts it triggered, of--what if? He really couldn't imagine life without Winnie.

Though both of them were barely 19, they had been almost inseparable for the past 14 years. His thoughts dashed back to when they were five and entered kindergarten, and from that time on they just enjoyed being with each other. They lived only a half mile from each other on the reservation. Many, many times when one of the mothers would call her child, she would get two. They loved doing things together. They really preferred each others company more than being with others of their own gender. When they were playing in groups and there seemed to be a dividing that was occurring between the boys and girls, they would quietly leave. Naturally they got a lot of teasing, but they didn't care, because it really didn't hurt their feelings. The two of them developed an extraordinary closeness which in time was well-known all over the reservation.

Joey remembered how exciting it was when they reached their developing years, the feelings that emerged and how enriching it was to them. Their love for each other was rare. When they shared their bodies with each other, they experienced a naturalness that went beyond the excitement of high emotions. He remembered well that beautiful mid-October afternoon--the temperature was in the mid-seventies--truly an Indian summer day, and how both of them wanted to go to their favorite wooded area where they were always alone. He recalled how they felt extremely close to each other as they walked. The slanting rays of the October sun graciously bestowed its warmth, and the soft autumn breeze was a beautiful reminder of a perfect summer day. That was one special day.

Without words, as they lay in each other's arms in the soft grass, they both had experienced a heightened dimension of feeling unlike they'd ever felt before. Both knew that words were useless, for nothing so rich could ever be told or explained. They were in wonder. That reverie in thought was suddenly interrupted by the fear of possibly losing Winnie. Those thoughts kept creeping in, and he had a hard time dislodging them.

He recalled that neither of them was surprised when about three weeks later Winnie realized that she had missed her period. Then they realized that most beautiful event on that memorable afternoon had much more significance than they had originally thought. He remembered that in the beginning of their 18 year-old lives, how suddenly a whole new spectrum of living had unveiled itself to them.

Their talks about their future included some deep feelings that had never really been fully discussed before. They talked about Winnie's mother, Marge, how she had felt compelled to name her Jennifer WindSong, because her mother had found so much delight when her little bundle of innocence looked up at her, even before her eyes had begun to track. The feeling that Marge experienced was like the soft, refreshing summer breeze that delightfully touches the face as it floats gracefully through the trees. It was the kind of caressing feeling that trees must adore. Marge had liked the name Jennifer, thinking to call her Jenny. But as she looked into the purity of those beautiful eyes, she could only call her Winnie from WindSong. Winnie's mother had told and retold Winnie how she came to be called WindSong. Joey had told Winnie many times that she was like a delightful, refreshing sunny breeze in his life.

Joey recalled the many, many times how his mother, Mary, had told him how she had been compelled in a strong dream to name him Joseph Long-Seeing, because of the good that Joey would bring to others through a gift to long-see future events in the life of others that would be helpful to them. Joseph was chosen by Mary, because Joey's father, Ray, expressed the same qualities that she saw in Joseph, the father of Jesus. She saw in Ray those impressive qualities of responsibility, sincerity and love that she recognized in the husband of Mary as outlined in the Bible.

Ray worked off the reservation in a refinery 80 miles away and could only get home on weekends. Life in general is very hard on the reservation, but Ray provided well and felt fortunate that his family never lacked in material welfare. Ray's life was a sacrifice for his family, but he never felt he wanted to move his family off the reservation into the White world, because he knew Mary would miss the community life there.

Joey recalled how he had come to accept his long-seeing ability which was well known on the res. And some had questioned him if he could long-see their concerns regarding problems and issues they had. Joey had no control over what he would long-see for others, and never could he long-see for himself. But Joey did keep silent about a lot of things that he foresaw happening in the life of others around him.

Joey was born with a great gift, and he had learned how to handle it well. He learned that it was of no avail to say to another that something dreadful or something of that order was going to happen in a person's life. It just did that person no good whatsoever to hear such not-good-things beforehand.

These things Joey and Winnie talked about, and they had felt that they had been given a large responsibility by having a child that was consummated on that beautiful autumn day not long ago. They simultaneously felt that it would be wise to get married right away for many reasons. Each had been saving what they could for their marriage, Winnie by the house cleaning jobs that came her way without her seeking them, and Joey by his part time work at Don's

Auto Service located just a ways off the res where he had worked since he was sixteen. They wanted to have a little nest-egg to start with, but they realized they would have to rely on what they had already saved. So they agreed to meet with Reverend Ron to discuss wedding plans.

Joey remembered how well Ron helped them by giving them full liberty to say their own words of love for each other. Ron was in total agreement with their wedding plans, as he considered himself just an officiator. He knew he couldn't marry anybody, that people were already married to each other by their love.

Ron, as everybody on the res called him, came to the res by a circuitous route. He had a difficult time getting through ministerial school because he didn't really believe what they tried to teach him about Jesus saving people from their sins. But somehow he got through and was ordained. He had served at two churches in his denomination, but in each church he didn't preach what the members wanted to hear, so in both churches they let him go before two years had passed. Ron always talked about what an outstanding man Jesus was and that everyone could always rely on His help at any time. Ron's message was always simple and uplifting, but it never rang fully with the picture of Jesus saving people from their sins.

Before Ron was let go the second time, he had a dream of a church, the picture of which was indelibly impressed upon his mind. He didn't understand the meaning of the dream until after he was let go. Then he began to see that the church he dreamed about was possibly his next church. But how was he going to find it? There seemed to be from Ron's point of view a million churches in the U.S. How to know where to begin to look was a conundrum, so he decided not to beat the bushes by looking conventionally, rather he would let information regarding the matter come to him. And sure enough, in a couple of weeks a fellow minister who was in his ministerial class, contacted him and they talked. His friend had told him how he became interested in Indian ways since ordination, and that he could contact an Indian friend of his who had been in his congregation but had moved away. Not really believing this was a lead to his new church, Ron decided to make the contact with this referred friend anyway. He had nothing to lose. When he did make the contact, he learned of an open church on an Indian reservation, which wasn't exactly what Ron had in mind. When he thought about the Indian church, he felt compelled to check it out. So he made the trip by car to the West coast and was able to locate the reservation, and lo! and behold!, the church was exactly the one he saw so vividly in his dream. He was so amazed he couldn't believe it! Of course the tribal council was ready to accept him, for the church had been in need of a minister for some time. Ron was able to secure some financial support from the administration of his denomination, so things took shape for him.

Ron had been with the reservation Indians for about eight years. They liked the message he gave about Jesus being their friend, and Ron liked their communal ways, and became good friends with many of them. Subsequently, Ron found he was being invited into many of their homes.

Ron knew of Joey and Winnie and was eager to help them. Ron was considered by many as one of them, because he fit in so well. This type of acceptance of others is quite common on the reservations, because equality of others is natural to them. Reservation life, while having its outer appearances of extreme hardship, Ron found to be rich in its community life. People know each other in ways that the White world does not.

Joey's thoughts turned to how fortunate he and Winnie were able to live rent free in his aunt's ten-foot-wide old mobile home which was only a few blocks from his own home. It wasn't much but it was clean and had good energy in it. His aunt had never married, but had been highly respected for carrying on much of the traditional ways of healing by her familiarity with herbs, and had taught many how to effectively use them. He was thinking it had been two years since Aunt Margaret had passed when a nurse interrupted his reflections, saying excitedly, "Your wife is awake and in labor."

Chapter 2

The Unimaginable

J OEY WASTED NO TIME IN getting to Winnie's side. Her face was strained--her water had broken. He learned that this had all happened quite suddenly. He thought quite possibly that Dr. Ross had sensed the need to get Winnie into a relaxed state to let nature takes its course. Whatever caused Winnie to be in labor, he was mighty grateful. Something was finally happening. She motioned to Joey to take her hand, and squeezing his hand hard, she started having another contraction. Dr. Ross said strongly but not harshly, "Push harder." The contraction ended, and almost as soon as it ended, another contraction came, and she pushed hard again, and the little one was born. After a bit, there were some deeply unintelligible sounds from the doctor and the nurse. Neither Winnie nor Joey could tell anything from those muffled sounds. Those quiet first seconds were deeply suspenseful, and the seconds ticked on with no sound from the newborn. Joey could feel his heart pounding. Something was definitely wrong! His thoughts were racing! Why couldn't he hear the baby cry? He looked at Winnie and he read the same anxiety on her face. This was not right!

Before they knew it, the nurse left the room with the infant bundled in a blanket. Dr. Ross prepared himself as best he could before emerging from behind the birthing screen. Finally he appeared, and with a terribly distressed look, he had to tell them that their child had been stillborn. He said that was possibly why her original contractions had stopped, and he offered his sincerest apology. Joey's heart sunk to the floor. Still holding Winnie's hand he gripped it ever so tightly in the gentlest way he could. Both let their tears fall. It was Joey who finally said, "We'll get through this somehow, sweetheart." Tears were now streaming down both of their cheeks. Another nurse came in and asked if there was anything she could do for them. They shook their heads no, and so the nurse left them to themselves. It was way too early for words; they had to let their emotional loss flow out.

After several minutes, Joey tried to gather his composure through his devastation and said softly, "Somehow there is an answer to this loss, dear, and it'll come to us. We must trust in all that's right. We've lived in the best way we've known how to live. I cannot see in any way that you or I are at fault."

With those words through her tears, Winnie looked at Joey, "You're right, sweet, I was thinking the same thing. Somehow, we'll know the reason why our baby didn't live."

At that moment the nurse came in and asked if the hospital had their permission to examine the baby to see if anything could be learned that might prevent this from happening to someone else. They looked at each other and nodded yes that it was okay. Another nurse came in and started to clean up, saying that the doctor would be back in a few minutes to look Winnie over to see if she was okay to be released.

When Dr. Ross did come in, he was as compassionate as a doctor could be. He found Winnie to be fine, and said that a staff member would be in presently to take their orders for food, and said she could leave in a couple of hours when she was feeling rested and felt strong enough. She had been through a great physical and highly emotional ordeal. Joey felt a tremendous relief that Winnie was okay.

Their lunch came and they barely felt like eating, but they ate as much as they could, and after a while Winnie felt a little better and said through her heavy tears that she'd like to leave. They weren't going to be able to get over this heavy blow anytime soon. Joey said that he'd bring the truck he had borrowed from Russ around to the entrance to pick her up.

About a month earlier Russ had met Joey at Don's where Joey worked and asked how Winnie was feeling. It was then that Russ offered Joey his truck when it was time to take Winnie to the hospital. Russ really liked Joey, for when Joey was only 13, Joey had gone to Russ' home to tell Russ that he had seen an immense cloud of smoke that obscured the highway that he knew Russ drove on his way to work. In a sincere emphatic way, he warned Russ not to drive into that dense smoke, that there was a big pile up of vehicles in that smoke and that two people were killed in that pile up.

Russ got up a little late the next morning and was hurrying so as not to be late, when he came up over a high rise in the road to see smoke covering the low area ahead. Seeing the smoke triggered what Joey had said. Slamming on the brakes, he pulled quickly to the side of the road, backed up as far as he could, jumped out and ran up the hill waving his arms frantically for motorists to stop. A couple of cars didn't stop, and he heard horrendous crashes coming from within the smoke. He finally managed to get cars to stop. Then he heard sirens. The stopped cars all had to turn around and take another route. Deeply shaken, Russ' heart was full of gratitude to Joey for having alerted him to avoid what might have been his death in such a pile up. Such was his weakness during those moments of deep reflection that he had to lean on his steering wheel like it was all that was supporting him. Evidently, atmospheric conditions had been just right for the smoke from the big brush fire that had been burning for three days to fill that low area of field and road. The news of Joey's long-seeing got around the res quickly. For some time afterwards, people on the res would smile a knowing smile to Joey.

Joey saw Winnie get out of the wheelchair and get into the truck. Her movements seemed to be natural without strain of any kind. He thought what a wonderful gal to be physically able to move in an okay manner. They had agreed that the hospital would call them regarding their baby.

They were pretty quiet. Joey did ask her if there was anything she wanted before they got home. She just shook her head no. Both had their heavy-hearted grief to deal with. To be going home childless without any understanding or explanation was definitely something unimaginable. A lot of wondering how-come thoughts crossed their devastated minds on the way home. Joey intended to drop Winnie off at home. He would then take Russ' truck to his house and walk back to their house alone. When Winnie learned that, she said no. She thought she could walk the four blocks home. She didn't really want to leave Joey's side, such was her painful grief. Joey's presence was all she had to hang onto at the moment.

When they came to Russ' home and turned into the drive, Russ' father was in the yard; he came over to them and asked how the baby was doing. Joey in a rather weak voice had to tell Joe that their baby had been stillborn. Joe felt a deep striking twitch within himself, for he felt a strong bond with Joey for having saved his son's life. All Joe managed to say was that he was deeply sorry, and asked if there was anything he could do for them. Joey replied no and thanked him. Saying goodbye, the two started walking the four blocks home.

They were pretty silent. They had walked slowly about a block, both of them gazing downward deeply downcast, when they heard the loud piping whistle of an eagle. They looked up to see not more than 30 feet above them a gliding bald eagle circling above their heads. They watched almost unbelievably as the eagle tightly circled three times above them. The eagle was so close they could see the yellow in its eyes. As the big bird flapped its way upward, it piped again its shrill whistle.

They both looked at each other in bewilderment! Had this really happened, they wondered? They were astonished to say the least! Both knew in their culture that the eagle meant the carrier of good news from Great Spirit, even though there was hardly any talk of their cultural ways and remembrances anymore. Life was pretty dull on the res without interactions of spiritual ceremonies and get-togethers.

That knowledge somehow had been lost in history through the encroachment of White man's reckless indulgence in developing a materialistic culture. The herding of tribes onto reservations had just about eliminated the possibility of providing the diet that they were accustomed to. This nullified their cultural ways causing them to lose interest in the ways they could no longer live, plus the White world was bound to try to change the Indian way of living to the way the White man lived. Thus a culture of people who lived with a deep reverent respect for all of the natural life around them, became almost totally lost. Any group of people who would be so cut off from their way of life, would fall into despair. Anyone looking upon the Indians as a whole from the outside would by appearance not see the true Indian as they used to live or know the true race they respectfully are. The judgments that followed made the Indian appear to be much less than those who judged them. Not much was voiced about this on the reservation, for such talk could not provide any inspiration. There was a despair that could be felt, and most all of them continually lived in it. To talk about it only tended to bring on resentment which most everyone shunned.

Thoughts of the eagle put them into a whole different plane of energy. When they resumed walking, they couldn't help but smile as they looked at each other. They had to accept what they had just seen. That eagle wasn't high in the sky; it had been right over their heads. There was no mistake that their eagle sighting was just for them. Had it not whistled its appearance and also whistled its departure? They were in big wonder! Their sighting definitely lifted their spirits even though they could not guess why such an event had happened to them. It seemed like they had entered a life of total mystery. Why had their baby been stillborn, and now what was the meaning of this wonderful eagle sighting?

They had walked about a block in their bafflement when a sound came from Ron's church. It sounded like a baby's cry. They both looked toward the church and heard it again. Then they saw it. A tiny basket had been placed next to the front door of the church. They wasted no time getting there, Joey careful not to go too fast for Winnie's sake.

When they looked into the basket, they saw a tiny white face. Automatically they both made exclamatory oohs! and wondered who would leave a precious little White one on the doorstep of a church, and above all, on an Indian reservation? What was that poor woman thinking? That was unimaginable in both of their minds. Winnie's heart went out to that poor woman, fully knowing what that loss must mean to her. Joey looked around but he couldn't see anyone. They had been so deep in their own sorrowful concerns that neither of them noticed anyone. Winnie wondered how long the baby had been there. She looked at Joey, and Joey read her mind. He picked up the basket by its handle to take the little-big surprise home to give it the care it needed. They couldn't help themselves. At that moment, they were the only ones around who could care for this helpless little one.

Their pace was different now. Even Winnie was moving more carefree than she had previously. Her heart was certainly lighter. Joey could hardly believe that this was happening. He hadn't had time to put all this together yet. There were just too many amazing things happening all at once. In the course of less than four hours they had more than enough gargantuan surprises for one lifetime. That it was overwhelming to Joey, was putting it mildly. Winnie with her motherly instincts kicking in was equally absorbed in wonder. She just couldn't fathom how a mother could let go of something that was so much a part of her. The basket was not a cheap one and the baby was wrapped in a nice blanket. A lot of attention and caring love must have gone through the mother's mind. This recognition of the mother's great loss caused an urge within Winnie to try her best to help this little one whose mother, for reasons unknown, had to let her baby go. This deep feeling of responsibility probably only a woman would understand. They reached home quickly. Now a new life would begin.

CHAPTER 3

TRUE SON--UNPRECEDENTED DESTINY

BOTH GRANDMOTHERS HAD SEEN TO it that the newborn would have all the tiny things that newborns need, so Winnie and Joey were well prepared with everything, only they had absolutely no idea that anything like this would happen. It was really a strange new something to get used to. Not only did they have to deal with their own heavy grief and loss, which included burying their stillborn respectfully, but they also had to extend themselves in all the directions needed to care for this beautiful but strange new White arrival in their lives.

The first thing that Winnie thought of when they walked in the door--when was the last time the little one had eaten? Winnie had already lactated some into her bra, so it was just natural to see if the little one would take her milk. Joey watched as Winnie opened her bra to let the little one find her nipple. They watched as the little White face readily found Winnie's dark nipple and began sucking away just as naturally as if he--it was a he they noted from changing his wet diaper--had nursed a hundred times before. Winnie exclaimed in joy, "Just like a true son!" With that automatic outburst they both looked at each other! Could that be what they would call him? As if they knew each other's thoughts, Winnie asked, "Do you think that's what we should call him?"

Joey was beaming, "I think True Son is a perfect name for him!"

There was never a thought that either one of them had that they were not going to keep this little one that had suddenly filled their devastated lives with so much unexpected love. True Son being White seemed to add a dimension of feeling that otherwise wouldn't be there if the baby was their own biological offspring. This good feeling of having a White-skinned son was baffling to Joey, but he wasn't going to try to figure it out. The feeling was so good he was just going to enjoy it. Winnie felt something too, but it wasn't as powerful with her as it was with Joey. To be sure, each had a lot of heavy feelings to deal with, and all of it would take some time for both of them to sort through. But, all in all, happiness was shining through both of them. After True Son had burped, he was soon fast asleep in his own bassinet. They agreed that it was time to tell their mothers. Winnie called her mother first, and she came in almost a minute. Joey's mother had been mighty anxious also, and she too joined them quickly. Both mothers were quite dumbfounded when the whole story was laid before them. And so began what the grandmothers thought was great news, and it spread itself like wildfire around the reservation. Nothing like this had ever happened on their reservation before, so the story got lots and lots of attention.

The first thing that Joey and Winnie had to do, was visit Reverend Ron and get his direction for what legal course they had to take. The next day when Ron heard the full story, he automatically said, "Surely, God works in mysterious ways His wonders to perform." Right off, intuitively he told them, "I believe there is a lot more to your experiences than it now appears. I really don't think there are any legal hoops that you will have to jump through. You know, there is no legal jurisdiction that can be made off the reservation regarding True Son. I'll try to make inquiries around in some stores and places off the res to see if I can find out anything about anybody abandoning a baby. Because I'm white, I won't draw any suspicion. Also, I'll ask Jim to nose around to learn if anyone saw a car near the church, or if anyone was seen with a basket near the church." Jim was the reservation officer, and he had his hands full with teenage drinking and drug use and with others who also had drinking problems. After a few days, all efforts to learn anything about the mysterious person who dropped off an infant on the church doorstep, came to naught.

It was the fourth day that Joey and Winnie had True Son. By this time the two of them had discussed a lot about what care True Son needed, for they had already concluded that a lot more needed to be known about raising True Son--the big thing, how would they provide the kind of education that True Son would need. They had already accepted that True was an auspicious child. And the buzz around the res about the White infant was of that same nature. Quite unexpectedly that day, Joey had a long-seeing experience that revealed the great work that True Son would be doing, not just on their reservation, but for all the Indians on all the reservations along the Western coast and also the huge impact that True Son would have on the White population as well. It was a huge revealing, and Joey felt a heavy responsibility as True's father in wanting to provide True with the spiritual guidance he saw so vital for him to have. Joey thought, where in the world would he ever learn all he needed to know spiritually to do that? To him that seemed like an impossibility. He didn't really consider himself to be spiritual at all. He barely accepted the spiritual reality of the extraordinary eagle sighting that he and Winnie had experienced.

When he shared this long-seeing experience of True Son's destiny with Winnie, she was not surprised. Great things are sometimes disclosed between the infant and the mother while nursing. Maybe it was osmosis between True Son and her, because Joey's long-seeing simply confirmed what she already knew. She further assured Joey that somehow he would be able to be there for True with the ability and the spiritual knowing of how to guide their son.

For Winnie it was very simple. Great Spirit had brought True Son into their lives by a series of irrefutable spiritual experiences, and she had a deep trust that both of them would be provided with what was needed to raise True in the spiritual manner that was necessary for his spiritual and cultural development. Joey felt what she was saying was so, and that relieved his concern somewhat. Still, how was he going to know things of the Spirit, when he presently knew he knew nothing?

Along with the joy that had come to both of them by this wonderful providential addition to their lives, also came huge expansions of new ideas for which neither of them had been prepared. This was reeling, particularly to Joey. Winnie seemed able to accept these mind-widening expansions much easier than Joey, no doubt because of her delightful demeanor of joy that everybody felt in her presence. She was already living the spiritual life in a most natural way. She was just naturally being the spiritual goodness that she was. Great Spirit had chosen an ideal mother for True Son. Joey hadn't realized that, but he was now beginning to see what a beautiful spiritual partner she was. He was seeing her inner strength come forth and taking charge like it was the most natural thing for her to do. Seeing this "more" of his true Winnie increased his love for her in ways he never expected. He always considered himself very fortunate to have Winnie by his side, but seeing her in a new light made him all the more grateful. The thing that made for harmony in their lives was that even with all her good strengths, Winnie was never pushy or forceful in any way. She was truly a very delightful wind song in his life.

As the days passed with Winnie and Joey adjusting to their new responsibilities, which greatly lessened the ordeal of their own personal loss, things were happening in the lives of some of those on the reservation too. Particularly significant was what was happening to Charlie. Charlie was a well-known alcoholic. He drank excessively to drown his burdening sorrows that took hold of him when he lost his wife, his dearest treasure. Life was tough for him on the res, but his life was eased by the great love he had for his wife. They had a wonderful relationship, and Beverly was really his life. When she succumbed suddenly to cancer, he was devastated. It seemed that she had no complaints of previously not feeling well, so there had been no chance of detecting the cancer earlier. It was one of those rare cases. When all the tests had been made, the doctors had to sorrowfully tell Charlie there was no hope for Beverly. Her body was too full of cancer.

In desperation, Charlie had gone to see Joey's mother to learn if Joey with his long-seeing ability could see if there was any hope for his wife. Mary invited Charlie in and called Joey, and the question was put to him. Joey feigned that he couldn't see anything, and being only ten he explained as best he could to Charlie that he wasn't in charge or in control of these long-seeings that came to him, and that he was sorry. He was sorry that he couldn't see a healing for his wife. Charlie left deplorably downhearted.

Actually, Joey did see his wife dying, and that was a hard thing for a ten-year-old to handle. But Joey had already come to know that it did no good to add bad news to what a person was already experiencing. He saw a lot of things that he had to keep to himself. His long-seeing ability was not exactly easy to handle, and it was not easy to have to keep this information to himself. He had learned that when he shared those sad revelations with his mother and father, it did neither of them any good to know the hurtful long-seeing things that he knew people were going to have happen in their lives. He had found that it was too hurtful to them to know those sorrowful things, so he had learned to keep silent about those heavy things that he foresaw. Each time that happened, he had to learn to let go of them. He had to. He just could not be happy carrying all that sorrowful information around with him. He had learned that those things were not really happening in his own life and that it actually could not affect him, so he was pretty much able to let them disappear from his mind. It took extremely clear realizations to gain that clarity.

Charlie was pretty drunk when he was told the story of how the White baby had come to live with Joey and Winnie, of how their own child had been stillborn and the eagle sighting announced their finding the White child to replace their own lifeless child. Even through his intoxication, Charlie got the full meaning of the message. The importance of the message caused him to sober up. Something happened to Charlie. He didn't want to drink anymore. He just felt a movement within to clean himself up and clean up his long-neglected home. Pretty soon he was out talking with others about this wonderful happening on their reservation.

People couldn't help but notice the big change in Charlie and were amazed how he spoke so caringly about Joey and Winnie. Charlie began to suggest to others that maybe they should have a meeting to talk about what was to him the biggest thing that ever happened in his life. So he knocked on doors and posted a notice in the community hall. People did see how deeply Charlie was affected by this happening, and they in turn were affected by Charlie. Word got around about the big change in Charlie, and most everyone felt a get-together would be a good idea. So in about two weeks from the time Joey and Winnie found True Son, people did meet wanting to talk about True Son, for word had traveled fast on the reservation.

Charlie had never conducted a meeting before, so he just opened the meeting up with a question, asking how they felt about a White child appearing in their community. Little did Charlie know that his simple way was organizing the true feelings of his friends in order that more questions could be asked at subsequent meetings. A consensus was forming there was more to discuss. Someone suggested they have a potluck at the next meeting. Everyone thought that was a good idea. They decided on a date and time. Charlie said he was going to try to clean up the community center, for it hadn't been used in a long time. Others volunteered to help him. It turned out to be a very successful meeting.

Chapter 4

The All-Enfolding Light

It was early September, three weeks had passed since True's arrival, and Joey was just about to leave work when one of the customers asked Joey if he wanted a lift home. Joey declined and thanked Tony, a regular customer. Joey needed some time to try to get clear on some things about how he was going to be there for True in a helpful way. Don could see the concern on Joey's face, for something that was that big on Joey's mind was not easy to hide. Don knew Joey to be a very deep person, and Don knew there was no way that he could be of any help to Joey. When Joey had turned 16, Don offered him a job because he liked Joey. Joey had hung around Don's Service Center quite a bit and had made himself useful many times. Don would have hired him sooner, but the restrictions in the state's safety laws for minors, wasn't a feasible option.

It turned out that hiring Joey was a very wise thing to do for his business. Joey was always pleasant with customers, sometimes seeing dangers beforehand that he saw occurring with customers' cars of which the customers were not aware. At such times he would tell Don about what he was seeing and would ask Don if he shouldn't question the customer about his car. That way, Joey didn't directly make his long-seeing known to the customer. It turned out that approach worked quite effectively for the customer. Joey was an asset to Don's business.

But mostly Don was grateful to Joey for making him aware of his daughter's diabetic condition of which neither he or his daughter was aware. Louise cashiered a lot for her dad, so Joey knew her well. He was surprised one day when his long-seeing saw Louise falling to the floor and passing out in a coma. He told Don about how he had seen her being very hard to awaken and thought she might have a blood problem. Don, knowing Joey's ability to long-see, wasted no time in getting his wife to make a doctor's appointment for Louise. It turned out she was diabetic enough to be prescribed to take insulin. A couple of years had passed since then, and Louise was feeling very well by having her diabetes under control. Prior to her diagnosis she had been feeling way out of sorts and didn't know what was wrong.

It was getting toward dusk and Joey felt he should pick up his pace a bit in order to get home to help Winnie in any way he could, plus he was hungry. He was only about a quarter of a mile from work when he automatically kicked a two inch rock that was just right for kicking, a left-over thing from having been a boy. As his foot squarely made contact with the rock, he was suddenly immersed in a tremendously brilliant white light. Instinctively he closed his eyes and brought his arm up to shield his eyes from this unexpected brilliance, but found the light still there in spite of having his eyes closed, and what's more, he could see right through his arm! This really made his heart beat almost to the point where he could hear it. He was totally alarmed! Everywhere, everything was brilliant light! He could see the surrounding bushes and trees filled with shimmering light, brighter than the light was elsewhere. His mind had no understanding of this. He just couldn't think; he had nothing to relate to. Just when he was about to think he was going crazy, he saw two little five-year-olds who were also in light, playing and chasing each other. That jerked him back to a sense of normalcy. By this time he had gotten somewhat used to the brilliance. He noted that he didn't see any shadows around anything visible to him. He found that he could see great distances almost as far as he wanted to see. Plus he was beginning to feel an extraordinary love for everything that he was seeing. The light was unfolding its immeasurable love. He was awestruck to say the least. Never in his wildest dreams had he ever heard or known of anything like the love he was now experiencing.

Then he noticed three Beings dressed in Indian garb of some sort, standing about 30 feet away. The three of them were more brilliant than anything else he was seeing. They raised their right arms to greet him. He didn't know what to make of them. Then he heard one of them speaking to him, not audibly from outside himself, but clearly and distinctly in his head.

The voice began, "**We are your friends from long ago. The light you are seeing is the Light of your own soul. You have desired deeply to know how you were going to spiritually help your new White son, which is why this experience is being given to you. Treasure it deeply. In time you will have the full understanding of what it means by letting the meaning reveal itself to you. Do not try to force it. At any time you can contact us, and we will come to your aid. We will always be close by, so you are never** alone." With having said those comforting words, they began to fade, and subsequently the light faded also. Joey was back in his own world. He had to sit down. He saw a stump in a yard not too far away. He made his way to it and was grateful that his legs held out as long as they did.

He didn't know how long the Light experience lasted. It wasn't much darker than he remembered it being when he kicked the rock. Love for everything was still lingering which made the experience all the more real. It was a love a thousand times greater than any love he had previously experienced. The love that was pouring from his heart was more than exciting--it was thrilling to say the least. In this love everything he looked at was the same powerful love. All he could do with his mind was be very, very grateful for such an astoundingly superb experience. This was a knowing experience he would cherish forever. Gradually the love also faded to where he was just glowing from it. What an incredible experience!

He felt somewhat normal again, so he decided to try walking as dusk was settling in. As he walked along, he found his steps seeming to be somehow lighter, almost as if he were gliding along. It was an easy feeling, not quite effortless, but almost. It was quite exhilarating actually. He thought deeply what he had been told by his visitors, grateful that he now felt he knew something that was tangibly of Great Spirit. Then it flashed across his mind that those whom he saw that were in so much light, must be the Elders that he had heard others speak of in times past. Wow! he thought. That's powerful! And they had said that they were always close, which made him feel like he and Winnie weren't so much alone in raising True Son. Joey felt like he was in a whole new world. There was much that he felt he needed to understand about the light, the love and the Oneness he felt with everything, but that would have to come in time. He could hardly wait to share with Winnie.

It was dark when he turned the door knob to let himself in. There was Winnie burping True before putting him down hopefully for the night. He wasn't sleeping through yet, but they knew that time would come. In the first three weeks, True had been a very good baby, eating, sleeping, eating, sleeping. He was a joyful little one to be caring for. Life was happily moving forward in a natural growing manner. The newness was wearing off. For such a great change in their lives, they had adjusted quite well.

Winnie took a quick look at Joey. She saw he was glowing--he had a radiance about him that was quickly noticeable. He stood there with a big smile that wouldn't let up. Before she could get the words out, "What are you so happy about?"

Joey offered, "I've just had the most extraordinary experience!" Winnie listened carefully with all her heart, absorbing all the feeling Joey was sharing with her. She was truly amazed. Whether she resonated with Joey's amazement or whether it was her own, it was hard to tell. For Winnie it was like Great Spirit had become full blown in their lives in a very real way, for she could feel in Joey's words something powerful that comes maybe only once in a lifetime. She became excitedly happy like Joey was happy. Sharing such powerful spiritual experiences on their level of deep love for each other had a remarkable fullness to it for Winnie. She was fully open and could feel all of it to a similar degree, making it real for her as well. Plus Joey's joy deeply affected her too. It rubbed off so easily on her that she became overjoyed too. It was Joey's joy to share those treasured moments with his one love. He would always remember how he felt One with Winnie as he unfolded the wonders of his heightened Light and love experience. Now that he had released his deepest feelings, he noticed the aroma of food that was coming from the kitchen. Winnie had been waiting for him, and so they sat down together to enjoy a fantastic stew that

Winnie had made. Joey thought "Life really doesn't get any better than this."

In the couple of weeks that followed, it became obvious to almost everyone who met Joey that something had happened to him. People on the res wanted to know how little True Son was doing which gave them the opportunity to talk with Joey when they saw him. While doing so they noticed that Joey's looks had changed. They noticed something more complete about him. He seemed to carry himself with a greater strength. He seemed happier, friendlier and his words seemed very honest and sincere. And so word got around about the change in Joey. Joey didn't know just how his experience in the light got around, but it did, and it gave the community a lot more to talk about. He felt like he and Winnie were under a microscope now. They shared their personal feelings about their new notoriety, particularly since the two meetings in the community hall were all about them. They came to the understanding that they had to accept what was happening, as the community felt that their lives had been affected to a great degree by True Son's arrival. There definitely was a growing wonder in the air that seemed healthy for the reservation.

For the first time in a long, long time, people felt like they were involved in something that was good for their reservation, and they had an eagerness to join together and be a part of something good, though they knew not what that was. It wasn't surprising that during their third community meeting, Charlie knew of a few who were independently drumming, so he asked how everyone felt about including some drumming and some singing in their get-togethers. Everyone was for it, but one asked how this could happen when their tribal knowledge wasn't remembered by anyone. Mike, an older man, volunteered that he knew a good song leader from a nearby tribe who might come and teach them at their next get-together. That was agreeable with everyone, for all felt that drumming and singing would add a lot to their potlucks. So a date was set for the next get-together. Charlie wondered if he could get Joey to share something about his Light experience at the next get-together. He would see. He felt that he should approach Joey alone on this personal idea, for he didn't want to build up expectations that couldn't be fulfilled.

Chapter 5

Another Big Surprise

It was Charlie's surging, compelling energy that corralled the energies of others to begin having get-togethers. At each potluck more people attended because of the magical wonder that the arrival of True Son introduced to the reservation. It was like the res was waking up from a lifeless, empty spell. Nobody could put a real finger on why the social life of the community had reached that dull state. It had just dwindled away. But now a new energy was present that could be felt from the combined energies of everyone as they came together practically of one accord. A new spirit on the res was taking hold. Joey could feel it when he was talking with people, and also when he and Winnie talked with their mothers.

The vitality that Joey felt was like the res was coming to life. People seemed to be much happier than before. And it felt good.

Neither Joey nor Winnie was yet aware that the news of True Son was reaching the ears of some in other tribes. The news was of such a high nature that its marvel couldn't help but spread to other tribes. It definitely was not a secret that could be kept. The marvel was taking on a life of its own.

Charlie was not aware of this as yet, nor was anyone else on the res aware of what was happening. Charlie felt that if Joey would share his Light experience, it would be a big benefit to everyone on the res. He felt compelled to ask Joey as he felt compelled to make the first meeting happen. What was compelling Charlie, he had no idea. He never questioned the feeling at all. It was just something he had to do. He had let go of his need to drink, and with every passing day he felt better. He felt like he had been resurrected to enjoy a new life with a lot of meaning in it. His innocence was infectious. Joey had heard about Charlie's life-change and was very happy for him.

It was a couple of days after the last meeting when Charlie got up enough nerve to ask Joey. Fortified with the feeling that this was the right thing to do, he took a chance that Joey would be home. Charlie felt relieved when Joey opened the door to his knocking, and it was the first time Charlie saw Joey since he and Winnie brought True Son home. Charlie was trying to find the right words and finally said, "Sure is good to see you, Joey" and words of thanksgiving just poured out of Charlie's heart for the change that had come into his life through their having found True Son and for bringing him home as their own. Charlie couldn't keep the tears back. Tears of gratitude had been waiting to flow for a long time.

Joey was quite affected by this sudden display of warmth. He asked Charlie if he wanted to come in, and Charlie acknowledged that he did. Once inside Charlie told Joey that no one knew that he was there to ask the question that he was about to ask. Charlie said there were a large number of people wondering about his Light experience, and had he ever thought about sharing that experience? Charlie went on to say how he thought it would be helpful to everyone, because he felt so strongly that it would be really good medicine for everyone to hear. Charlie was surprised at his using the words "good medicine;" they just slipped out. Joey was quite taken back by Charlie's request. He hadn't ever thought of speaking about the light. He thought the experience was just for him and Winnie. He never dreamed of going public with it.

He was just about to tell Charlie that he didn't think he could do that when the voice within his head said, **"Be not afraid to share what has been given you, for it needs to be shared. People are hungry for the Light. Just speak from your Heart."**

Joey was stunned. He asked Charlie to sit down, because he needed to sit down too. Joey was visibly shaken and Charlie could see it. Charlie said, "Joey, I didn't mean to upset you. I'm really sorry." With that Charlie started to get up, but Joey waved him back down.

Joey thought, what was the best way to tell Charlie yes? There's no way he could tell him what he just heard. Finally Joey said, "I was going to say no to you, but the strong thought flashed across my mind that light is what people might need right now."

Charlie beamed. He knew deep within himself that was true. Charlie proceeded to tell Joey of the get-togethers and how people were benefiting from them. He told him the time and when the next get-together was going to be held, and he told him that he didn't need to bring anything. There was plenty of food for all. Charlie left soon, leaving Joey in wonderment.

Winnie came out when she heard Charlie leave and asked what that was all about, because she couldn't catch all of it. Joey told her everything; how Charlie's tears flowed in gratitude and how deeply moved he was by Charlie's sincerity. The word that was going around about Charlie's sobriety was true. He confided in Winnie that speaking in front of a lot of people was fearful to him. Winnie didn't know what to say, but she ventured, "You'll do all right. The right words will come to you, and they'll be honest, true words." He saw the rightness of what she said, and that helped a little.

Joey didn't know if he was up to any more challenges. In the last five weeks he could barely keep up with the adjustments he had to make in his thinking. His consciousness had really broadened in a very short time. Now he had another future date to think about on top of what he was still digesting from his overwhelming Light experience, which in addition of trying to understand all that had been revealed to him, more questions about spiritual matters continued to enter his mind. And, of course, more realizations continued to flood in, giving him more to think about. It seemed there was no end to the spiritual awakening he was having, although he still didn't consider himself to be spiritual.

Don had noticed a big change in Joey too. He had heard some time ago about Joey and Winnie's new family, but never really pried into Joey's personal affairs, because he could see Joey's deep brooding mood. Don also had heard about Joey's Light experience. Joey's new life was really getting around.

Don's heart really went out to Joey, and it dawned on him that he could really help Joey. When Joey arrived at work the next morning, Don greeted him with a smile asking, "How long have you been working here?"

In addition to Don's smile which was unusual, Joey thought Don's question to be a bit unusual too, and replied, "Over three years. Why?"

Don answered, "Well, Joey, I really don't think I've paid you enough. I just couldn't afford to give you more. To make up for it, I want to give you my '85 Toyota. I've got two other trucks around here, and I don't need three. You've driven the truck many times. Do you think you'd like to have it?"

Joey could hardly believe his ears. "You're not kidding me, are you?" he asked half believing Don's offer.

"No. I would never kid around on something like this." Don replied. "I've got the title all filled out. Just give me a dollar to make it all square and legal."

Joey was dumbfounded! He didn't know what to say. That's what he told Don. He just thanked him over and over again, all the time wearing a huge, delightful smile that didn't want to quit. Joey couldn't believe this had just happened. He was amazed that Don would give him his truck! It was the nicest looking of the three trucks Don had. There was nothing wrong with the truck. It ran well. It was clean for 70,000 miles. There was just a slight crease in the tailgate; other than that, it was a good looking truck. Wow! he thought, Great Spirit must be smiling on him. With the baby they really needed a set of wheels.

Joey gladly signed the title, and with a lot of fun gave Don a dollar, and both went out to look at the truck. Don said, "I'll tell you what, Joey. It'll be too hard for you to work today. Why don't you take the day off, and I'll pay you for it. That way you can enjoy yourself with Winnie and your baby and maybe take them for a little ride. The tank is full. What do you say?"

Again Joey was flustered. Don said, "You don't have to thank me. You've earned this, and I know you really need some transportation. Now, don't waste any time leaving. We'll just have to get along without you today."

Joey stammered out a big, "Thank you." got in and drove off waving goodbye. Could he really believe this was happening--his own truck? But he really was feeling the joy of driving it, so the reality of it was beginning to sink in. He could never have imagined this in a million years. His heart was singing like it had never sung before.

He pulled into his yard, and with one jump was out of the truck and in the front door, and yelled, "Honey, come quick."

She yelled back, "In a minute." Shortly, she emerged from the bathroom, "What's all the fuss about?"

Joey opened the door and said happily, "Look!"

Winnie looked and said questioningly, "So-o?"

"It's ours! No kidding, it's ours," he fairly chortled. "Can you imagine? It's ours."

All Winnie could say was, "Really?"

Joey said, "It's really ours. Don just gave it to us, and he gave me the day off with pay." Now it was Winnie's turn to digest what seemed to be a heaven-sent gift. Winnie leaned into Joey with her arm sliding around his waist and his arm went naturally about her shoulders. They just stood there embraced in wonder looking at their new truck. Ever since they were married, they really needed some kind of a vehicle, and here was a nice looking truck. She was just as surprised as Joey had been. This was a surprise that would take some time to fade away for both of them. To suddenly have transportation was more than delightful. When you have practically nothing, it was way-over-the-top happiness.

What a joy it was to tell their mothers they wouldn't have to borrow their cars any more. Both mothers were really happy for them. The mothers were somewhat mystified too at their sudden turn of good fortune. It was the kind of news that would brighten anyone's day.

When the excitement quieted down and Joey had time to think of something else, his thoughts returned to what had been burdening his mind. He noted that for the last several hours he had not felt the heaviness that attended those thoughts that he had of having to speak before a group of his peers. It dawned on him that if he could keep from thinking those heavy fearful thoughts, he was truly fine, kind of like remembering how he had to let go of those long-seeings that were really not a part of his own life. He wondered, was there a trick that would relieve him of the dreaded idea that paraded itself across his mind continually of having to speak to a group? Was there some way to keep those persistent, fearful thoughts from appearing in his mind? He hadn't tried to contact his Elders yet. He wondered if his Elders could help him. He remembered their words--*just speak from your heart*, but still the fears persisted.

By and by, when he looked at his fear thoughts, Joey saw those fears were totally of his own thinking, and that he could choose to think other thoughts. To him that was a huge revelation! Those fears were of his own thinking! How simple! He saw that everything in life was how he thought about it. This was an amazing realization! If he didn't like what he was getting from the thoughts he was thinking, he didn't have to think that kind of thought any more. Why hadn't he ever tumbled onto this before? It was like waking up from a big dream. He had seen this very clearly. He knew from then on that he would have to watch his thoughts all the time, for he didn't like bad feelings. Wow! He could control his life!

When he looked ahead to when he was to speak, Winnie was right. He could see that the right words would come if he spoke from his heart honestly. There really wasn't much to fear in doing that. His honesty would support him; he was sure of it. In just a few minutes of seeing clearly, a big load was lifted from his mind. With that heaviness gone, he felt much lighter and freer.

Once again joy filled his heart. He had a truck! He decided to see if there was any part of his eight-year old truck that needed spiffing up. Everything looked pretty fine; he didn't even need to wash it. Over lunch they talked about taking a short ride just to celebrate the newness of it. They waited until after True's next feeding was over, bundled him up and did just that. It was one delightful ride. Life proved to be more independent and less complicated for them from then on. Their hearts overflowed with gratitude to Don.

Chapter 6

Light Expands Into the Reservation

THERE WAS A BUZZING EXPECTATION going around the res when it was learned that there was going to be some drumming and singing and that Joey was going to talk about his Light experience at the next get-together. Mike had been more than successful when he made contact with John about teaching them drumming. The word had also spread on John's reservation how a couple came to adopt a White child that Great Spirit had given them to replace the loss of their own child. That news was causing great wonder as it spread throughout all the reservations. John told Mike that he would like to bring others with him to sing their songs as they drummed on their grandfather drum, because John was feeling this was something special they wanted to do. Learning that, Charlie's excitement was contagious! Charlie didn't know it, but their Community Hall was going to become quite small. Now everyone seemed to be interested. There was an excitement in the air. Nothing like this had ever happened on the res, at least no one could ever remember anything like it.

Joey had no long-seeing of anything like this happening. He could see that drumming and singing would simply be good for everyone, for it would prove helpful to regain their cultural ways, and that would breathe more and more new life into everyone. He was beginning to feel like he was being a part of something that was much larger than him alone. And, of course, Winnie picked up on what Joey was feeling, so they soon learned that they were not apart from the accelerated tempo of reservation life. For the last six weeks or so, they had been fully occupied with their own expansions in life, not to the point of isolation exactly, but they had felt being somewhat apart from what was happening in the community. Now they were starting to feel a vibrant connection to what was happening socially on the res.

They had no awareness of how far-reaching that vibrant social activity was underlining the possible spiritual awakening that was going to occur.

So the early autumn days passed before the next get-together. A tang in the air was heralding a colder season ahead. Some canned the rewards from their gardens, while others busied themselves getting their winter wood supply in. But there wasn't the same-old, same-old way of doing those seasonal necessities as in times past. Now there was anticipation in the air to get things done, because there was a greater interest filling their minds. There was more alertness regarding the possibilities what the next get-together would bring.

There were two or three that consistently drummed with each other, but why others didn't join them was unknown. They were delighted to learn there was an emphasis on drumming at the next potluck. Others were eager about it too, for they were feeling something strong was awakening within them.

Some were finding their drums that hadn't been used for a long time. A few could remember trying to drum by themselves, but had to give it up because the feeling wasn't there when they drummed alone. For most of those who found their drums, they remembered the good feelings that came as they sensed that their drumming was like listening to Great Spirit's heart beat. They felt the deep respect for the tom-tom or tum-tum and were gladdened that this sacred instrument was going to be a cherished part of their get-togethers. So it was not surprising that those who had drums brought them when the day of the get-together arrived. It was hardly an auspicious occasion, but there were plenty of heightened feelings. People seemed excited to be with each other. Some met friends they hadn't talked with or seen in quite a while. So this wasn't just a meeting; this was a real get-together. It seemed that the more that came, the more pronounced were the good feelings that were felt.

Get-togethers with the members of a tribe heightened good feelings because of the deep common community interest they shared with each other. It was dramatically different when compared to the heightened feelings of a church fellowship. That could be said because of their tribal commonality; they all brought a beautiful energy that contributed to the whole of all the feelings of those present. These hard-to-describe get-togethers are a vitally important function on the res. Where get-togethers have strong spiritual participation, they form the life blood of the tribe, which greatly augments the spiritual life of the participants. So almost without an undue effort on anyone's part, wonderful get-togethers were spiritually stimulating.

Mike was talking with Charlie when John's van pulled up with his companions. Introductions were made, the grandfather drum was unloaded carefully and the potluck contributions were all carried inside. John wanted to know, "Was Joey Long-Seeing here yet?" because he wanted to see what the 19-year-old looked like who had caused such a stir around. Charlie replied that he'd be here shortly. Mike and John busied themselves catching up on their lives, and Charlie introduced his new friends to those already inside. There was plenty of interest when other tribal members met members from another tribe. Plenty of "Do you know so and so?" It was lively as the hall began filling up. When Joey arrived there was a cordiality shown to him that he never experienced before. Joey sensed it was going to be a big evening for him.

The potluck dishes were splendid as almost all potlucks are. Charlie began by asking Mike if he'd like to introduce John and his friends from the next reservation. Mike's warm introduction of John and a little of John's drumming history started the evening off with warm expectations. John said that he was very thankful when Mike asked him to come, and there was no way he could not come. It was always a deep pleasure for him to help expand interest in drumming. John told of how he had been drumming since before he was eight years old, how he learned tribal songs in his native tongue from his elders some 65 years ago. And then he said, "I want to start with a song that means, I'm happy to live the Spirit life." With that, John started drumming on his tum-tum and opened with his beautiful, melodious baritone voice. It was a real pleasure to listen to the rise and fall of the tones as they penetrated one's body cells. The words were in Salish, the common language of most tribes along the coastal waters, but each had their different inflections that caused dialects in the language. Then John asked, "How many drums do we have here tonight?" Over twenty drums were lifted up. "Let's drum." And everyone followed John's beat for a few minutes as John offered another song with his companions joining in. People were feeling the drumming energy. It was moving them. They were getting a feeling of what they had been missing for a long time and had almost been forgotten.

John said, "And now as an introduction to Joey whom we are all waiting to hear, my friends and I would like to sing a song to Great Spirit using our grandfather drum, and so began the rhythmic beat of five drumsticks beating in unison upon the deep sounding grandfather drum accompanied by a chorus of strong male voices that honored Great Spirit. Everyone could feel it, and when they finished in about five minutes, John signaled to Charlie. Charlie thanked John deeply, saying that he hoped they would sing again afterwards, to which everyone clapped a resounding yes. Charlie then turned to Joey and said, "Thanks for coming, Joey. Everyone appreciates your being here with us." He then motioned Joey to begin.

Joey was pretty nervous. He had looked around and he thought that he was perhaps the youngest one in the room. The thought flashed through his mind that he had no business talking to a group older than himself. And immediately the strong thought took over that *age had nothing to do with what he was going to share.* So letting go of ideas about his young age, he began by telling everyone he was nervous, that this was his first time speaking to a large group. He said that this was something they didn't teach him in high school, which drew a little laugh, which made him feel a little easier. He thought he should ask if anyone hadn't heard the details of how True Son came to live with Winnie and him. The five visiting drummers raised their hands as did a few others. And so he told the whole story from start to finish. Some found that his version differed a little from what they had heard circulating around. But that's the way circulating information sometimes gets altered when passed around from person to person verbally.

Joey started by saying that he knew why everyone wanted to hear about his Light experience, as it came to be called. He said,

"We all have questions about why we're living here on a reservation in such difficult living conditions. We wonder about a lot of things that we don't have answers to, and that's because we don't really know that we are Light, not just a tiny light, but that we have our whole Being in light. It's been barely three weeks since I had my Light experience in which there was nothing but light, and I'm still learning from it. I'm really feeling very premature being here tonight saying to you, 'You are Light.' It's just that all of us have forgotten who we really are. To have an experience like what I've had, is more real than the chair you're sitting on, the air you breathe and the body you're wearing. Did you know you wear your body? You wear your body because you are Light, and light has to have something in which to experience in this world. The idea is to never think that you are just a body. You are Light wearing a body." I've had this idea continually coming to me for three weeks now, and each time this thought is in my mind I feel a warm gushing love in my heart, which is why I'm here sharing with you tonight. I want everyone to feel this amazing truth."

He continued, "I was walking home from work and dusk was settling in, when very suddenly everything became brilliant light; there was no place where light was not. Light was shimmering in everything that was alive. Light was in the pavement, the sky and everywhere else. Light was far brighter than the sun at noon. But greater than light is the cause of light which is love. I take that back, for light and love are the same. Let's just say that light is love made visible; not love as we know love for earthly things or for loved ones, but love that's more than a thousand times greater than any love we've ever known. And this great love manifests itself as Light. This love was pouring out of my heart, and it generated an unbelievable satisfying feeling unlike anything I've ever experienced. I knew this love to be life itself. When you have this love pouring itself out of your heart, everything you see is that same love and not just the objects you are looking at. Love gives meaning to life as we all know, but this spiritual love is life itself. Without love, we know that we shrivel up and life has no meaning; we're destitute of life. In this same manner, our lives are totally incomplete without this spiritual love of the heart, which is why we have so many problems in life. Great Spirit love is really all there is.

"I'm brand new at trying to share what is very difficult to put into words, so bear with me if you're not understanding what I'm trying to convey to you. I never had any intention of sharing this experience publicly, only with my closest ones. I feel very inadequate in trying to find the right words, so please bear with me.

"Right now I feel this love flowing out to all of you, and it makes me feel like we're all connected together. This love flows out of my heart of its own accord. I really feel that it has all the intelligence of knowing exactly the right thing to do. I have come to realize that I cannot be me and be this dynamic love too. So I have chosen to be love, which means that in order to be this love, I have to give up control of thinking that I am in charge of my life. I know that it is Great Spirit that is trying to live its life through me as the love that it is. And I know what is true for me is also true for you. You are far greater in Spirit than you realize.

"Joey isn't any different than you. (Now it seemed that he, Joey, was not doing the speaking.) All are of One Spirit, having many different faces. Each of you is endowed with the life of your Creator. It never could be otherwise. Cultures have come and gone from the face of this earth, and in the course of time, all in those cultures never really knew of their true existence, which is why your histories have been marked with so much violence and hardships. What you are hearing tonight is that at any time you can turn within, and the truth of who you are will be revealed to you. Your true spiritual Self, Great Spirit, always stands ready to welcome you back home to your true life of being all you can conceive of being.

Each of you has a wonderful Inner Life that far exceeds anything you've ever dreamed of. You will find this Inner Life in your own heart. It is the knowledge that all of your great ancestors tried to keep you focused on."

With the ending of those words, Joey was left in control of speaking. He said, "I see that was quite a mouthful. Maybe we'd better stand and stretch a bit, and then I'll try to answer any questions that you might have."

Did he just say that? He didn't know what possessed him to think that he knew what they didn't. The offer to answer questions had been made. It was too late to renege.

When the meeting resumed, the first question asked was, "Joey, we all know that from time to time you've helped some on the res avoid a catastrophe by being able to see ahead what could possibly happen to them. It seems odd to some of us, why you weren't told beforehand that big experiences lay ahead for you and Winnie. Wouldn't it have been easier if you had known beforehand what was in store for you?"

Joey thought and said, "Well, it might possibly have helped in some ways, but honestly, I never would have liked to have known that our baby was going to be stillborn. And if I had tried to prepare myself beforehand to know that I was going to experience the light the way I did, I might have altered my experience by my thinking about it in some way. Who knows? I prefer to let experiences come as they will. I have never been able to see ahead for myself, although there have been times when I've wanted to, but that has not been Spirit's way. In the same manner, I cannot order any moments of long-seeing. I'm just an instrument for Great Spirit's use."

The next question he thought was getting a little personal when the questioner asked what he thought was going to be True Son's mission for their tribe. A confirming murmur filled the hall. Evidently, a lot of people were wondering the same thing. Joey answered, "I don't really know myself. We'll just have to let time reveal what that will be, if anything." Joey thought that all the speculations about True Son really should cease. He was an infant, and it seemed that he should be raised in a normal manner. But he was not about to tell people how they should think, which is why he kept his answer brief. But he did add, "True Son is White, and we should treat him as if he is one of us. He is, after all, a son of this reservation." That seemed to satisfy the questioner and Joey was thankful, for he was able to express his feelings without countering anyone.

He looked at Charlie who said, "There's time for just one more question--maybe something pertaining to the Light that you are." There was some light mumbling, but no one got up to ask anything.

Joey said, "If you don't have any questions now, some may come to mind later. If you want to talk later, your time is my time. Please feel free to talk with me any time." With that he said, "Now let's hear more drumming and singing to satisfy our souls."

Joey's words had made an impact to some degree upon all present. To some they were the words they longed to hear. For those, his words verified the treasured feeling they were holding inside themselves. Mainly, it gave most of those in attendance something to ponder on, and for a few it was a little far-fetched--way too far out of the ordinary. But one person who was deeply affected was Reverend Ron. Joey's words stirred something deep inside him. He would not be able to forget them. Then there was John and his friends who had to try to carry back with them what they had just heard. Joey had spoken from his heart innocently, which had allowed Great Spirit to empower some words that Joey knew that he was not saying of his own volition. An impact of truth had been made. Joey was happy when he had finished talking. That hadn't been too hard to do he thought.

The drumming and singing that followed added a dimension of closer feelings in the evening. Everyone felt uplifted. Mike would be in touch with John after learning what the people wanted to do about drumming. Charlie's intuition was right on; he had done what he felt he had to do. Because he was instrumental in arranging the affairs of the get-together, he could see it from an over-all perspective that others could not. He felt the fourth get-together was very good. Little did he realize that his pure mannerisms played a great part in making the get-togethers happen.

Chapter 7

Reservation Hunger

A COUPLE OF DAYS HAD PASSED after the get-together, and Joey had thought that people might have waited until they could ask their questions in private, but no one had made any contact with him. He began to wonder why, and as he continued to wonder, no answer readily came. He certainly could not fathom them not being more interested in knowing about having their Being in Light. It was puzzling. Maybe it was taking a long time for the message to sink in. After all, it took him some time to grasp the truth that he was Light itself, and he was right in it. Finally he let all his wondering thoughts drop away. So he was very surprised when Reverend Ron knocked on his door, asking if he could speak with him.

Joey invited him in and with his deep smile Ron greeted Winnie. Winnie exchanged friendly greetings with Ron, and excusing herself she got up to go into the bedroom. Ron said, "Please don't leave on my account. I'd like you to hear what's on my mind too, because I know Joey will share it with you later anyway. What I have to talk about is no big secret."

Ron began by telling them how deeply affected he had been by Joey's sharing of his Light experience, and that it had taken him this long to feel ready to discuss his feelings with Joey. Joey thought maybe he was right in thinking that others might have been really jarred too and couldn't put their thoughts together yet.

Ron continued by telling of his experience with Jesus when he was only 11 years old. "Jesus," he said, "came to me personally one day while I was sitting on the edge of a dock with my legs dangling toward the water in the lake. My house was nearby, and I often went to the lake just to daydream."

He said he was taken by surprise when this nice man sat down next to him, saying to him, "It's a nice day and a nice place to daydream." With those words, Ron said he felt an engulfing softness surrounding him unlike anything he had ever experienced. He said the man told him, "Ron, you're going to help a lot of people by being a minister." Ron said that at such an early age he had never thought of doing anything like that, and he found the man's words baffling to him. But the beautiful feeling that came from this man was being felt throughout his whole body, and somehow he believed this man's words. He said they both sat in silence for a few minutes, and finally the man said, "I must be going."

Ron said, "He never got up--he just disappeared. But I was still engulfed in that beautiful feeling which lasted for almost the rest of the day. I later realized that the man was Jesus." He said, "A knowing just came over me that it was Him. It was that experience which pointed me toward becoming a minister. I read the Bible a lot, but all the words seemed cold compared to the beautiful feelings of that experience."

As Ron told of his experience with Jesus, Joey felt chills running through his whole body. Winnie felt them too. Whether she felt them directly or she felt what Joey was feeling, it was difficult to tell. But Ron was affecting them both. The reality of his experience was causing a tingling in the air. Ron then told how it became almost like his mission to let others know how great a friend Jesus is to everyone, how he couldn't get swept up in accepting the idea that Jesus could save anyone from their sins, because he felt no comparison between that idea and what He personally knew about Jesus through his experience with Him, how he had a tough time getting through ministerial training and how difficult it had been to be let go from two different churches, because he wasn't telling them what they wanted to hear. He then shared how he came to be on the res. Joey was glad to hear Ron open up. It let him feel more connected to Ron. Deep things when shared break through outer barriers between people.

Ron said, "The reason why I'm here is to let you know that your deep experience of being in the light triggered something deep inside me. It reminded me of Jesus' words, *'If thine eye be single, thy whole body shall be full of light, but if thine eye be full of darkness, how great is that darkness.'* That's been going round and round in my mind, and I can't seem to understand His words. I am sure your words about our being the Light and Jesus' words are tied together, but I can't figure out how. Your words have caused me to really examine His other words that are recorded in the Bible. What has affected me so deeply is, that by your telling us we actually are Light, that has made me see that His words point to the truth that the Truth is who we are. This makes so much more sense than the idea that He is the only one with a divine origin." Both Joey and Winnie were nodding their heads yes.

Waiting to see if Ron had anything more to add, when he didn't, Joey said, "Yes, I can see now that such a huge idea being totally different than everyone was believing themselves to be, can almost cause a paralysis in one's thinking. To tell you the truth, I had been expecting people to be knocking on my door, but they haven't. Your sharing your concern has really opened my eyes. Have you tied anything together how my Light experience ties in with Jesus' words that you quoted?"

"Not really." was Ron's reply. "I don't understand what He meant *'if thine eye be single?'* We have two eyes, not just one eye."

The idea flashed through Joey's mind that the single eye meant the eye of mind, how we see with our mind. He told Ron how he had realized that one's whole destiny could be controlled by thinking right thoughts. That one's thoughts had everything to do in life with what a person was going to experience. Joey told him about the fear he had of speaking before a group who were a lot older than himself, and how he had suddenly seen that all he was looking at were his own thoughts, and that he could change them. Then he said, "It really looks like Jesus was saying, "If we can keep our thoughts on a single subject like thinking that we are Light and love, our whole bodies will be filled with light. Does that make any sense to you?"

Ron's eyes brightened, "Yes, I see what you've just said to be true. That really does make sense. You know, in this new light, I'm going to really study Jesus' words. He also said to, *'Seek the truth, and the truth shall make you free.'* He told us also to, *'Seek first the kingdom of God...'* It sure is obvious now that I fully see His words from a different perspective. He meant to seek within ourselves, Joey. It suddenly makes perfect sense. We can't be anything else other than love and Light." With that, Ron laid back into his chair smiling and said, "To think, all these almost 40 years I have thought that heaven was out there someplace." He couldn't get over how revealing it all was to him. It all seemed so logical and coherent. It seemed to take his breath away, because he realized that his life was going to be totally different from then on.

Joey could identify with what Ron was feeling. Joey's life had completely changed too.

Joey, seeing a need for an interruption asked, "Ron, how about a cup of coffee?" Ron nodded, and Winnie rose to make some. The air wasn't heavy, but coffee would ground all of them a little. Ron really felt fortunate that he could share his deepest thoughts with Joey and Winnie. He wondered, how many times do people have such a rare opportunity to share so deeply. Small talk around coffee had a settling effect upon everyone.

Now it was Joey's turn to tell Ron how grateful he was that he shared his concern with them, for his own understanding was enlarged too. He had never really read the Bible, but knew that people all over the world believed in what the Bible said in one way or another. Joey said he didn't feel that he needed to look into the Bible at that time, because he was still having expanding realizations from his Light experience. He thought to himself that it might serve as reference material later on.

That was the beginning of a big enfoldment of the truth within Ron. It seemed that he needed that one revelation to set off a string of spiritual revealing experiences within which put new life into Ron. Those who attended his services noticed an increase in Ron's understanding that tied in with Joey's light experience. In addition to being fed the high quality of Jesus always being a helpful presence in their lives, his listeners were gaining insights regarding their own Great Spirit Essence. It was not by chance that Ron was led to pastor on the reservation, for he was totally in league with Joey's consciousness, and between the two they were stirring the hearts of many on the res spiritually.

Joey wasn't asked to share at any of the get-togethers that followed, but he was happy to attend them. He too felt like he was more a part of the reservation life than before his Light experience. His love for everyone filled his heart to overflowing, and he just shared his heart with everyone.

From time to time others did knock on his door with questions looking for clarity. He could see that he wasn't providing all that people were looking for in regard to their desires to return to their cultural ways. Joey had provided the deep incentive for them to become enlivened to their spirituality, but he knew he couldn't provide everything. He was a big blank on his own cultural ways. So he was thinking to talk with Charlie about what he thought, for he knew that Charlie had his pulse on what the people were feeling. True, the desire to drum and sing was taking hold with John's help, but Joey wondered what more could be done. When Joey talked with Charlie, Charlie said, "Let's find out."

At the next get-together, Charlie posed the question, "What more would you like to see of your past ways that would give more meaning to your lives?" Joey thought--how simple. Charlie's magnetism was at work again. The consensus was that there was a need, but no specifics were voiced. It was suggested that as many as could, attend Pow-Wows that other tribes sponsored in the summer months ahead. Those real get-togethers featured a lot of drumming groups, personal dancing and inter-tribal dancing that generated high cultural feelings. Everyone thought the openness of the plan was good.

What Joey sensed, and what others were really wanting to know once again, was their connectedness or Oneness with all the natural life around them. Ever since the Red Man had come to big Turtle Island, as many of the ancient ones from the northeast called this North American continent, they had to learn how to subsist within their environment in order to live. They learned that to destroy any part of the land and anything it contained, tended to destroy themselves, for they depended on the life around them to provide them with their food and other living needs, which is why when the Whites were unscrupulous in how they abused and wasted the natural resources of the land they were conquering, they could not fathom the ignorance of the White Man. The White Man's ways were far different than the Red Man's living respectfully with all surrounding life.

With well over 60% of the Native American population having moved off the reservations at some time or other to find work and live in cities, those left on the reservations look on sadly how civilization is destroying itself, which compounds their hopelessness. Wanting to return to live their cultural ways is the feeling on all reservations. In a troubled world, they are looking for sanctity in their lives. Whites don't consciously know it, but at their deepest level, they know things aren't right either and they desire sanctity too. The rightness in the depth of souls does bleed subconsciously through to the outer surface.

It had been about six months since True Son came to be with Joey and Winnie, and there was a hum, a quickening of life that had come to the res. So it was like a bolt out of the blue when Joey got a call from John asking, did Joey think that he could come to their next get-together? John said there had been a growing interest in his tribe about Joey and Winnie's White son and in Joey's Light experience. John also wondered if Joey could bring his wife and son too. Boy, Joey thought. He would have to give this some thought, and he would have to ask Winnie what she thought. He told John that and said he would get back to him in a couple of days. He got John's phone number and said he thought it nice of John to want him to come to their get-together.

When Joey told Winnie, both knew there was a lot to consider. Word from others on the res had reached them about how the news had spread to other reservations. So they knew they had created quite a stir in the tribal communities. Joey wondered out loud if he had an obligation to share what he had thought was just for their reservation. Was he up to doing that? To him it was a big question, because he could see that if he said yes to John, there was the likelihood that other tribes might also want him to share with them. Winnie's concern was equal to Joey's concern. She thought deeply about it, and finally she said, "You don't have to make a decision right now. Why don't you let the idea rest for a day or so, so that we can consider all the possible effects of what this would mean by saying yes or no. Then we will be able to discuss what it is that you want to do." Joey agreed.

To Joey, this was not something that he could think about later. To him this was huge, and what about Winnie and True Son going too? He supposed that eventually his brothers and sisters would all want to look upon the face of his White son. But he didn't want True to be some kind of side show, and he certainly didn't want a big fuss made over him. He wasn't concerned about True being white and growing up on the res. There were a number on the res who were of mixed blood. Some looked like they were all Caucasian. So True being White didn't really concern him. It was the amount of undue attention that he might receive. Maybe he was not perceiving clearly, but he did want to be protective. Was True old enough to be in large crowds? They had taken him to the last two get-togethers and he had been okay. Still there was the drive to think about. He would leave that decision to Winnie, because most of the prep and care of True would be in her lap.

He thought about his obligation to share his Light experience. He saw that thinking about it was not going to get him anywhere. Somehow, automatically, he just began to gaze into the matter like he would gaze into glowing embers in a fire. That way, surprisingly, he could see the whole picture of what he was contemplating. He saw the profound impact that the sharing of his Light experience had on others, which made him realize that he could not back away from sharing his experience when he was sincerely asked to do so. He had accepted the fact that light was what every person was hungry for, and he had no right to deny the truth to anyone that they are Light. If sharing the light was in his future, then that was the direction his life would take. It wasn't what he wanted to do with his life, but he knew he would have to follow Great Spirit's leading. Knowing that he would say yes to John felt like a heavy load had been placed on his shoulders. Maybe the reason it felt so heavy was because there loomed in the future more of the same requests from other tribes. He would just have to get used to it. Then he thought about how his thoughts affected his life, and right away he saw that he was going to have only one speaking engagement at a time and not a whole bunch of them at once. His fearful thoughts had wanted to run away on their own, but his awareness prevented him from fantasizing upon what was not yet happening. Joey was learning to control his thoughts.

He shared with Winnie how he had determined to say yes to John, how he could not refuse the sincerity of John's request. She had thought that would be his decision and she agreed with him, adding, "I feel certain that to say no, we would have a lot of guilt to deal with later." Joey nodded in agreement.

Joey asked what she thought of her and True going along with him. She had given that a lot of thought too, and said, "With an hour's ride to and from the res, and that the weather was uncertain at this time of year, it might be too much of a challenge for True with their getting home much later than his bedtime. He was just starting to sit up alone; it seemed too much to put on his good disposition. If it weren't winter, it might be different." He knew she was right, but his preference was that he would like them to go with him, mostly as support, although that was hard for him to admit to himself.

Chapter 8

Awakening to the Light

I N THE NEARLY SIX MONTHS since that Joey had spoken at the fourth tribal get-together, it was not the same Joey that would be speaking to John's tribe when he would say yes to John's request to speak to them. Joey had expanded greatly in spiritual knowing. Joey's learning to control his thoughts had greatly lessened the number of thoughts that flowed through his mind. By watching what he was thinking, Joey found that a great many of his thoughts were extraneous thoughts that added nothing to his life. By seeing those extra thoughts for what they were, he uncovered their unreality to his life, and seeing them so clearly, those thoughts no longer occupied his thinking life. They just dropped away which resulted in having a beautiful peace of mind that he'd never known before.

Joey wasn't fully aware that the peace of mind he was gaining was actually helping to increase the expansions which were unveiling the natural reality of spiritual life that he found so intriguing. Expansions or inner revelations to his mind were coming to him so fast that he had barely enough time to fit each one into his understanding before the next inner revealing expanded his knowing further. He surely was not trying to force anything that his Elders had warned him against doing. There seemed to be no let-up in what his Light experience would reveal. Having Winnie to share his inner revelations with, was just what the doctor ordered, so to speak, because he had to put into words his new understanding, which further anchored the reality of the experience. Thus he was gaining a deeper comprehension and Winnie was gaining in her understanding also. Each revelation was like a spiritual light bulb going on.

What Joey was seeing in the overall, was how the outer life was blending into the inner life of the Light that sustained it. Without the Light, he saw there would be no outer life. He came to see that the two were actually one. He knew that to be solidly so, because when he experienced the love that radiated out from his heart, everything his mental gaze fell upon was that same love. And what was even more beautiful, there wasn't any separation of anything in that love. Everything was love. He saw that neither love nor Light could ever be divided, no matter what thoughts anyone might think to the contrary. The Reality of Light and love was superior to anything the physical senses might report back to him as the observer.

Joey saw how limiting the physical senses were. Eyes could only see what appeared visually. The eyes and the other senses are there to relate to the physical world. Joey now knew that the conscious mind with all its thinking, was the processor of all the information that the senses brought to the mind. Joey was beginning to understand that the mind's main function was to process information, that it could not of its own accord come up with anything new about life.

Now he was beginning to understand how his ancestors blended in with all their natural surroundings so easily. They allowed the animals, the trees, the water and the plants to teach them their ways. What his ancestors learned from the surrounding life, they processed with their minds, thus they could live with the surrounding life naturally. Joey was learning how his ancestors respected all life because all life was a vital part of everything else. And in that knowing he saw how his ancestors were grateful for everything. His ancestors were an intrinsic part of everything in nature. They took from nature only what they needed, so they were never burdened with something they didn't need. How totally different that was from White Man's ways.

Joey was truly true-seeing, but how could he convey this understanding to his tribe when they were confined to a tiny bit of land that couldn't provide their needs? What's more, his ancestors didn't have money to deal with which this current civilization thrives on in order to function. For the first time he came to understand how artificial the White Man's world is. In the present scheme of things, neither the White Man, nor the Red or any of the other race of man has a chance to live differently. Man, through his taking and warring, had dug a deep hole and was seemingly pulling the hole in on top of himself. Joey could see that only the Light and love within each person could make the world better, that all other efforts were only patch work.

With this shared understanding, both he and Winnie began to awaken to the huge responsibility that lay before them. He would be going to John's tribe with a whole new perspective that was far beyond anything in his personal life. Again Joey felt that anyone who was nearing 20, was far too young to be given such a huge responsibility. He knew, of course, that he was not alone in trying to bring truth to a sleeping world; still, he thought he was pretty young to be part of the awakening that is so vitally needed. After all, he didn't even have a college education. He didn't have any credentials as the world viewed credentials. So there was a feeling of inadequacy in doing the task that lay ahead.

Again the voice in his head filled his mind with helpful words, **"Joey, you have the Light within you. The Light and love that you are, are all the credentials you need."** Those powerful words jolted Joey out of his inadequate feelings. He accepted his Elders' perspective. And he further realized that he was much better prepared with his increased understanding than he had been when he had first spoken. This sharing might even be fun. He called John to say he was coming to their get-together. He learned the time and got directions.

When he pulled onto the reservation it was dark, and he remembered how when kissing Winnie goodbye, she had said how she missed going with him. That fortified him all the way to the res. He saw a group of cars up ahead and thought that must be their meeting place. When he got inside and introduced himself, he was greeted with genuine warmth that he didn't expect. He was introduced to so many new faces, he knew he would never remember them all even if he tried. All the introductions were made so easily; it was very enjoyable. There was some drumming and a few songs that brought a settling tone to the atmosphere. The potluck was delicious and made him feel comfortable. Potlucks were becoming a favorite of his. He was enjoying the easiness of the atmosphere, almost to the point of forgetting that he was going to speak. Joey was relaxed.

John said they were only going to drum for a few minutes, as they wanted to give Joey all the time he needed to speak, as everyone was eager to hear him. So after establishing a feeling of tribal communion, John introduced Joey, saying how good it was to have him with them after what seemed a long time of waiting. Joey got up and began by saying how much Winnie had wanted to come, but felt that True Son was a little too young to make the trip, but Winnie did send her loving greetings to everyone.

Joey confessed that he felt somewhat strange by all the attention that he and Winnie were feeling because of their being given a White baby to call their own. He asked, "How many would like to hear how it happened?" Everyone raised their hand. He had thought it best to start with that question in order for everyone to know all the details. So Joey retold the whole emotional story of True Son's arrival. This is what they all had been waiting to hear.

Then he said, "I'd like to share my experience of being in the light. Would you like to hear it?" There was a nodding of heads and the strong murmuring yes could be heard. So Joey began by saying that True Son's arrival had caused a great concern within himself of how he was going to be able to be there with the understanding that would provide the right spiritual guidance for True Son, when he had no spiritual understanding at all. He could feel the interest in the audience growing, so he told the whole story about being in the light and how sequential spiritual love filled his heart to overflowing, how it affected him so deeply knowing that he was Light and that his true identity was Light and love and knowing that everyone was also Light and love. He said without reservation, "That experience changed my whole life, for I could never think again as I had thought before having my Light experience." The enrapt audience was silent. Joey could sense that they needed to move around a little, so he said, "Let's take a short break; then we'll resume. Maybe you might want to ask some questions."

When they were all quiet again, Joey began by saying, "We like participating in our ceremonies that bring back good feelings and memories of the life that we once had. I say this on behalf of all tribes, because there is longing in our hearts to return to a way of life that is no longer possible to live. The type of civilization that surrounds our tribes makes it impossible to return fully to the family culture of our tribes." There was a murmuring of approval. "But," Joey said, "that does not stop us from living who and what we are. Our ancestors knew that they were Great Spirit, and they had their ceremonies to help them experience the greatness of the Spirit they knew themselves to be. They knew the light and love that made them all One. It was their way of life. And in the same way we can know we are Light and love as they knew themselves to be. It is as simple as thinking that you are the Light and love of the Great Spirit, as you now think of yourselves to be a self which is not the truth of who you are. All of us have been blinded to think this way, mostly because this is the way the White world thinks. They have been the blind leading the blind, but I am telling you, you are not blind. You have the truth of knowing Great Spirit is everything in your life. No one has the power to make you think otherwise. We are waking up to our true identity."

The audience was a little stunned that Joey had put the Truth right in their laps. "Who has a question?" Joey asked. He felt they had questions, so he let the silence that followed his question continue until an elderly one rose from his seat.

"Joey," the elderly one said, "you say we are Great Spirit, that we are Light and love. How do we go about remembering that?"

This was just the lead that Joey wanted to hear, he felt primed. "Well," Joey said, "we all think thoughts, and we all know that how we think and what we think determines what we are going to experience in life. If we think gloomy thoughts, we are going to be gloomy. If we think happy thoughts, we are going to be happy. Likewise, if we think that we are just a self that the world cares nothing for, that is what we get--nothing. But when we acknowledge the truth that we are Great Spirit, that we are Light and that we are love, we elevate our thinking to the level that gives us new life. Believe me, we are not fooling ourselves when we think highly of ourselves. This true thought has a powerful effect upon our whole Being. It makes us feel much better and in time changes our whole life. Thinking we are Great Spirit is the truth of who we are. Why think we are less than who we really are? Does that make sense to you?" he asked the elderly man directly.

The elderly one replied, "Well, you've given me something to think about." Joey knew he had hit home within the elderly one. Joey wondered how many more he had clearly affected.

Joey said, "You know the Indian has a big heart. Potlatching (give away) is a big thing in Indian life. This heart, this very center of you is where potlatching, the sweetness of life, comes from. It is from your heart that the radiant love that you are flows forth. All it needs is a little help in getting the heart to open. And your thinking will do just that by claiming the truth that you are Great Spirit, that Great Spirit is your life, and this will let you give all of what you call your life to Great Spirit. By this desiring you too will experience the real truth of who you are. In this way you open the door for Great Spirit to act in your life." Joey didn't know what more he could say. He had given his kernels of truth to what he hoped were hungry ears.

Presently someone stood up and said, "You make it sound so simple."

Joey said, "It is all very simple. Great Spirit which each one of us is, is an integral part of us that wants to live through us. It knows how to fill our lives with its beautiful goodness far better than we ourselves know how to do. It knows goodness in ways that we do not, because Great Spirit is absolute goodness. It seems to me that White Man's culture has rubbed off on us, making us think that life needs to be complicated with a lot of thinking that really does us no good at all. As Indians who used to live simply with our natural surroundings that provided us with everything, life was really simple. We have lost our innocent ways through thinking, and this thinking has complicated our lives in a big way. But we can take back our lives and live simply in Great Spirit by letting It live us. Far greater is that than living in complicated thinking. Life itself is simple. Love and Light is not complex. Does that help?"

That one said, "That helped a lot. Thank you very much."

Joey was finding that all that he was saying was not coming from his mind alone. Somehow, words were flowing that he had not intended to say. But he was glad, for he recognized that the choice of out-flowing words was much better than he could have formulated by himself. He wondered if time was getting on. He looked at John who motioned him to keep going.

"Does anyone else have a question?" Joey asked.

A person in the back said, "I want to be sure if it's okay. I've been taping what you've said tonight, and I'm glad I did, because I know I need to hear it again. Is that all right?"

Joey said, "It's okay with me. My words are your property." Laughing he said, "I only wish they were everyone's property." A chuckling was heard. "Maybe it's time to wind this up." With that, he motioned to John.

John thanked Joey for coming and said, "We've all benefited by what you've said. I think we'll forego any more drumming tonight, for we have been filled in another way." It seemed a good idea to everyone. John made his way over to Joey and thanked him and gave him an envelope saying, "This will help you with your gas." Joey blinked in surprise, saying thank you with his eyes.

Five others presently came up to Joey, all asking if he would consider coming to their tribes to speak. It turned out each one was from a different tribe. Joey was flustered to say the least. Joey politely said he'd give it thoughtful consideration, because he would have to discuss it with Winnie. They all gave him their names and phone numbers and the tribes they belonged to. Joey thanked them for wanting him to speak to their tribes. That was one big surprise. Joey never thought anything like that would happen. It pretty much proved to him that there were many more that wanted to hear what he had to say.

Just as he had perceived, the word that had gotten around the reservations was not just something that was lightly floating around as a piece of everyday news. The news had captured a lot of attention. It was late and he thought he should be going, because he had to go to work in the morning. Many thanked him on the way out.

The drive home was quicker than it had been going to the res. When he got home, Winnie was sleeping. As he took off his jacket, he felt the envelope John had given him. He had forgotten all about it. He opened it up and there was $140 inside. It was a delight he didn't expect. His heart was deeply touched. He would have to call John and really thank him.

Being very careful not to awaken True, for he was sleeping through now, he lay down in bed. Winnie turned toward him and said in a sleepy voice, "Hi," and was soon back to sleep. Joey's eyes closed, but his mind was still actively reviewing the whole of the evening, until he thought, I can think about this tomorrow, and dwelling in gratitude for all the help he had been given, his mind relaxed and was soon sound asleep.

CHAPTER 9

CHARLIE'S GREAT EFFECT

H E HADN'T HEARD WINNIE GET up to feed True. When he was dressed, he came out to both of them beaming. As soon as True saw Joey he opened his arms. Joey picked up True, gave him a big kiss, twirled him around a couple of times and tossed him lightly into the air a few times like he always did. True really liked Joey's warm love, and in their growing bond, True was always eager to be in Joey's arms. Casting his attention Winnie's way, Joey began telling Winnie about how well the evening went, about all the nice people he met and how John had given him a gift of $140. Winnie's smile said that was nice. Then he told her of the invitations to speak to five more tribes. In one way it surprised her, but in another way it didn't surprise her.

She had thought this might happen, but didn't expect it to happen so soon. This was quite unexpected. Naturally, she asked Joey what he was going to do, to which he replied, "I think we need to talk about it."

They had both foreseen the probability of many reservations wanting to know firsthand about what was considered an auspicious happening by Great Spirit. They had accepted that. On many reservations, large questions had risen that primarily dealt with the magnitude of what the addition of a White son meant fortuitously to the whole of the Indian population. Many felt this to be a momentous happening. Whatever the feelings, a lot of questions were generated which is why they all needed to personally hear the father of this White son speak.

Joey and Winnie had sensed this coming and knew consequently that this was going to be a big undertaking that would form a natural part of their lives, although neither wanted their lives to change. They both felt reluctant in wanting their personal life to be infringed upon. And here it appeared that this was the beginning of what would inevitably happen.

It was Winnie who said, "Joey, this all looks so big to us right now. It doesn't look like we have any choice in the way our lives are going to go. It appears that we have been chosen to help our people and maybe a lot of other people by raising True Son in order for him to do his work in this world. Our time and energy is to do whatever is necessary for that to take place." Joey agreed. To him what had been divulging to be something of a spiritual work, was starting much sooner than he expected. This was the hard part--accepting that it was already happening. They weren't even out of their teens yet. Winnie spoke again smiling, "It's not happening right this minute, so when you get home from work tonight, why don't we go out to eat, enjoy ourselves and get rid of this sudden heaviness."

Joey nodded agreeably saying, "Good idea. There's too much to consider right now." And they did just that. For each it turned out to be a pleasant day.

The next day when they put their heads together, they concluded that with the possibility there would be more tribes requesting to hear him speak, they would need a map to pinpoint every reservation's location. They also felt it would also be wise to create a file to note pertinent information about each tribe. With over two dozen reservations, trying to remember details about, 3 or 4 tribes alone would be a challenge, but two dozen or more would definitely require a file. There was no telling if any of the information in the file would be useful later, but it seemed logical that it would be better to have a file than not have one. For this they thought they would need a computer, but for the present a paper file would suffice.

And they recognized the possibility that members from other tribes might contact them by phone when they learned that Joey was visiting tribes. They would also need a good calendar to keep things straight. And they never thought they were being presumptuous at all. They could clearly see the handwriting on the wall. They were trying to stay ahead of the game. That way they thought they would still retain some control over their lives. They also thought the question of remuneration for Joey's time might come up. Both thought that a free will offering would leave it open for each tribe to consider. Another thought occurred to them that it might be a good idea to put all the offerings that might be received into a bank account for True. They were bouncing ideas off each other, trying to see ahead, because the immediate future looked like it could get very busy.

Then Joey had to consider the reality that he wasn't capable of visiting more than one reservation a week, and that on his off day from work. Later they would come to realize that some reservations were so far away, it wasn't possible to return home that same night.

He would have to stay overnight. So, their new venture grew more complex all the time.

They got a map but found that they had to enlarge it to make it useful. So, nervously, Joey began calling the closest one first to arrange a speaking time. Setting up the schedule for each tribe took some time. When the five were scheduled, it looked a little awesome to Joey, but he reminded himself that it was only one speaking engagement at a time, which took the initial impact away and made it look smaller. He talked to Winnie, saying he was going to be doing a lot of driving and that it might be a good idea to check if a GPS might help to find the reservations a lot easier. He wasn't sure whether they were available for cars, but he would check with Don. She thought they could probably afford it.

Joey's life had quite suddenly become very full. Little did he realize at the time how important this experience was going to be when he needed to give True a broadening perspective on Indian life. He had asked how he was going to provide True with the education he would need, and he was to get that education in a way he didn't expect. This would dawn on him in time, for each reservation he spoke at was a warm, unique experience. He was to find as time went on that each tribal community had their own beautiful feeling that they generated. Joey was to get a feeling-education of good-vibrations, probably the best kind of sharing that could be shared with another. Joey was going to get an education of the heart, something that text books could never provide. It's the kind of education that rubs off on people by osmosis. It's an education that would broaden Joey far more than he ever dreamed of. And if Joey could know it, he in turn was making a great impact on people in all the reservations he visited. He was opening a big door for them to increase their own well-being. They were finding his words uplifting, which was giving them a greater purpose in life, something which they were in long need of. He was being instrumental in guiding them to feel their true spiritual heritage. In time Joey was becoming a household name, although he knew nothing about his charisma that was having such a large effect on everyone.

By summertime he had spoken at nearly twenty reservations, and True was growing fast and was now at the stage where he was always running, as little ones are wont to do in their exuberance of wanting to explore. Their ten-foot-wide mobile home was constantly becoming smaller as True accumulated more and more toys. Somehow, Winnie and Joey were managing in such small quarters. They had both grown up in homes with plenty of space, so being so condensed was not exactly to their liking, but they had no way of buying a larger home. They were making do with what they had.

One day Charlie stopped by and noticed how crowded they all were in their small home. From time to time when he would see True with either Winnie or Joey around the res, he noted how fast True was growing. It dawned on him that they needed a bigger home, and he knew that word was getting around of the impact that Joey's words were having on the tribes he had spoken to. He began to wonder--could it be possible to buy Joey and Winnie a new home? They certainly deserved it, and True Son needed more room to grow up in.

The idea began to percolate in Charlie's mind. It got so that Charlie wondered out loud his thoughts to others. Charlie didn't know it, but he was spreading the idea around. What Charlie was actually doing was waking up the compassionate side of his brothers and sisters who began to think like he was thinking. It was common knowledge that the arrival of True Son on the reservation and Joey's subsequent sharing of his enlightening experience was the good medicine the tribe needed. It had all made for an awakening of new life for almost everyone in the tribe, except for the teen-agers who were still having their drinking and drug use problems. They were still lost in their hopelessness of not seeing any kind of a future for themselves. With no cultural heritage there wasn't any direction. That, coupled with the lack of financial opportunities and the White world's materialistic enticements, it was extremely difficult for young reservation minds to see beyond what appeared to be huge walls locking them in. This was a common problem on many reservations.

People soon came to Charlie with their wondering of what they might do to provide Joey and his family with a bigger home. Charlie really didn't know what the first step was, so rather than saying he didn't know, he just said, "Let's sleep on it." Charlie did have an idea, though it seemed strange to him at the time. He would go to the teen-agers and ask them if they wanted to help raise money to buy a new home for Joey. He knew them and could talk their language, having been an alcoholic himself.

So he began sniffing around, visiting their drinking haunts. He found some of them, and they wondered what Charlie was doing talking to them. This was really the first time he tried to talk to his young friends for almost a year. He told them his story that he just didn't like to drink anymore, that he had awakened to a new life that they probably wouldn't understand. But he told them that Joey was such a good person that he and his family deserved to live in a larger home because they were doing so much good for the reservation. That was why he was telling his story to them. Would they like to help raise money to buy them a new home? This idea floored them! Was Charlie crazy? They didn't much care about anything or care much about themselves. And how would they raise money? Everybody would think they were looking for money to spend on drinks. And they told Charlie he was barking up the wrong tree. Charlie left soon after that, letting them think about what he had told them. Those friends of his went on drinking, but they were left with something to think about.

As time went on, they told Charlie's story to other teen-agers; they couldn't help themselves. Charlie's story wouldn't leave the minds of those teen-agers whom he had talked to. They had something to talk about other than where would they get their next bottle. Charlie had gotten through the blur and density that alcohol causes. They knew how heavily Charlie used to drink and how he hadn't cared about anything. They could see the great change in Charlie and could feel his sincerity in the way he told his story. What was it that caused Charlie to change? Charlie was like a different person. He seemed to genuinely care for people, and his caring had rubbed off on them. Their new interest in Charlie was sobering them up. Their new thinking didn't seem to jibe with their drinking. So they thought in order to know more and have their questions answered, Charlie was their best bet to help them understand better. Besides they knew Charlie and felt they could trust him.

Charlie heard a knock on his door, and when he opened it, he was somewhat surprised to see all five teen-agers looking a little sheepish. He could tell they hadn't been drinking, so he invited them in. One of them started by saying they all thanked him for coming to them and telling them his story. Now they were there to try to learn more of what had caused him to stop drinking. Charlie didn't expect his own story to have had that effect on them, but his healing had a great effect on many in his tribe. He was a spurring inspiration to many, kind of a catalyzing agent. And now his same innocence was at work again affecting teen-agers.

Charlie told them the whole story from start to finish, including the tremendous effect True Son and Joey's sharing was having on other tribes up and down the coast. New life was taking place in the hearts and minds of many Indians. The teen-agers listened attentively to all that Charlie said. They were trying to grasp the meanings, but their young minds hadn't ever heard anything like this before. Drinking had blurred their minds so much they knew nothing of what had occurred during the past ten months. It was big, even if they couldn't put it all together or understand it all. But it had changed Charlie, and Charlie's change was having an effect on them. It was all too much to handle all at once. They needed time to let it all sink in so that it could have meaning for them. They made some small talk and left Charlie, thanking him for his time and telling his story. Charlie said he was only passing on what had helped him, and that if he could help them further, they could talk to him any time.

Well, Charlie thought after they left, at least they weren't drinking, and they seemed genuinely sincere. He knew it was going to take some time for understanding to take hold. He didn't really understand why he had gone to them to ask them if they would help raise money to buy Joey and his family a new home. He had just done what he felt he needed to do. Charlie, unknowingly in his innocent demeanor, was being a true agent of Great Spirit.

Joey was pretty oblivious to what was taking place in the individual lives of others. He wasn't aware of any details in any personal lives. So, he was surprised when he opened his door one day to see Roger, an old high school friend, standing there with a beautiful young White girl. He had heard the strong knock and thought it was possibly a neighbor. Roger smiled at Joey and said it had been a long time since they had seen each other, and Joey smiled back saying that yes, it has been quite awhile. Joey had heard that he had moved off the reservation some time ago, and wondered what had brought Roger to his door. Joey greeted both of them and was introduced to Sally, Roger's girl friend. He asked them in.

In their high school years, Roger was three years ahead of Joey. Roger was a strong, outgoing personality who was always forward, bullying others, and much of the time he put others down in order to make himself look bigger. He caused so much ill feeling in others that many of his schoolmates shunned him. Maybe partly because

Joey was younger and he secretly liked Winnie who ignored his flirtations, he picked on Joey. One day when Joey was the brunt of his demeaning attacks, which really didn't hurt Joey because he didn't really pay much attention to them, Joey saw something. He went up to Roger and said, "Can we talk alone for a few minutes?"

Roger, thinking Joey was going to defend himself in some way and that he could have more fun with him said, "Sure."

So they went to a vacant area and Joey started to talk first saying, "Roger, you have a gun hidden in one of your drawers. It has a bullet in the chamber, and if you don't get rid of it right away, you're going to kill someone in your family. You won't be charged because it will be seen as an accident, but you will cause a lot of grief and sorrow that you will have to live with the rest of your life." He saw Roger's face drain, and Roger felt his knees go weak.

He thought, how could Joey know about his gun? That was incomprehensible to him because it was true. That the gun could go off accidentally had never occurred to him and it really frightened him.

Joey continued, "I really think you should carefully remove the bullet from the chamber and get rid of the gun as soon as possible. Otherwise there is the danger of forgetting what I just told you, and you will kill someone."

That changed Roger's whole day. He trembled within himself because of what Joey had told him in such a matter-of-fact fashion. After school, he did exactly what Joey had told him to do. Roger, afterward, thought reflectively with gratitude that his accidentally killing someone he loved could never happen now that he no longer had the gun. He could never look at Joey condescendingly anymore and could no longer berate others. Because of Joey, Roger let go of his superior feelings and became a really nice guy to be around. Joey was happy later to see Roger get elected president of his class.

Roger told Joey, "Sally and I have been going together, and we're feeling really close and we share a lot. I told her about how you changed my life. I never did thank you, but please know I have always been grateful. You made a big difference in my life, and I've always wanted to repay you in some way. Naturally I shared with Sally the incident of how I got rid of the gun, which has made her want to meet you. And when my folks shared with me about how your White son came to you and Winnie and how everyone has been so deeply affected by your Light experience, both Sally and I have wanted to pay you a visit."

Joey was always being surprised in some way, but this was big in the surprise department. And he told them it was a big surprise to learn that a White person was interested in Indian affairs. He also told Roger, "Please don't feel you owe me anything. It was something I saw that I needed to let you know about. If I had not told you and later learned that what I'd seen had come true, think how guilty I would have felt? I was just doing what I felt I had to do. I am happy that you listened to me. That's the only payment I need."

Sally liked what Joey had just told Roger and said in reply, "I really don't see much difference in the color of skin that people have. People are who they are regardless of their skin color." Now Joey was getting educated. Suddenly a barrier had been lifted. She asked about his son being named True Son. "How did that happen?"

Joey felt obliged to tell her all the details since she was a woman and could feel deeper than most men can feel. Both were pretty amazed. They felt they had not wasted their time in coming to see Joey. They were feeling an authenticity in the air; something intrigued them deeply. Sally asked about Indian life, "Do Indians live in different ways than White people?"

"This is a big question," Joey said. "Today the Indians who still live on a reservation have a yearning to return to their cultural ways of old in which they honored the land because it supported them with all their needs. They respected the wildlife around them, because they knew Great Spirit was what gave life to everything, the same as it gave them life. They felt connected to everything and knew the value that each life contributed toward what makes nature work. This is the life the Red Man can no longer live. His living environment has been deeply desecrated for the sake of making money. Today the Indian feels a great need to be reconnected to everything again to regain their feeling of Being One in a world that cannot feel, because people are trapped in their minds by false ideas that do not serve everyone in a fair way. Today's society does not know that they are, without exception, the Light and love of Spirit and not just a self which tries to find happiness in a world outside of themselves, as opposed to the actual knowing of the true ways that life should be lived in order to experience the true happiness that comes from the Light and love within oneself."

In amazement Roger said, "Say that again." It was more than he could understand in one hearing. "What you have just said is something like my parents have told me, only much clearer. They've been trying to tell me that your knowledge comes from having had a Light experience of some sort?"

Joey said, "Yes. The Red Man can regain his connection with Great Spirit by recognizing that he cannot be anything else but Great Spirit, because he is the Light and love of Great Spirit. He is more than just a Red Man, as is the White Man more than just a White Man. Both are of the One Great Spirit. Each is not different from the other. People color themselves in many ways by thinking they are something which they are not. All of us must learn that we are of the same One Spirit in order for the world to regain its long-lost sanity."

Sally had said nothing. She knew now why she had wanted so earnestly to meet Joey. She had heard wisdom from someone who actually knew what he was saying, and she knew his words to be true. Her understanding was coming quickly. She could see how Great Spirit had chosen him and his wife to be the parents of one who was going to follow in Joey's footsteps in helping people cast off their hypnotic spells and know the full truth of their Selves. She marveled at how simple everything really was. She had always felt there was a simple answer to everything. For the first time she saw clearly what life was all about. She had just awakened. Now with this sudden realization, she felt an eagerness to get on with what she was going to do with her life. She wondered if she was attracted to Roger just to learn from Joey or? She loved Roger a lot and had an easiness with him. Still, there were cultural differences to understand. These thoughts flashed through her mind, and she decided any questions she had could be answered in time.

Joey spoke saying, "Winnie is just pulling in. I want you to meet my family." With that, he went outside to help Winnie with the groceries. Sally got the chance to meet Winnie and True Son who was always ready with a big smile for everyone. Sally found True delightful while Roger and Joey talked. Roger told Joey he was driving big rigs with short hauls not too far from home, so he had somewhat of a normal life for a truck driver, which allowed him to spend time with Sally. He told Joey that he was just getting to know Sally and that she had many fine qualities, and that the White world was a lot different from life on the res, but he was learning. He also told Joey that what he had shared with them was helping him to see a much bigger picture of life than he thought life was. He said he had a lot to consider.

When they were all sitting down, Joey told Winnie that he had been filling Roger and Sally in with the story of their lives, and that they were probably still digesting what he had said. Winnie remarked, "Oh, and did he tell you that for the last six months he has been going to other reservations to share our story with them?" Roger and Sally looked surprised. They had no idea the news was being broadcast so extensively. Now Roger was really starting to take notice of Joey. Roger was feeling slightly overwhelmed that he was in the company of one whom he now thought was a high intelligence. He thought, it's no wonder he was named Joseph Long-Seeing. Now Roger had a lot more to think about. What he liked about Joey was that he was so natural. He thought he would like to be like Joey, easy and peaceful.

Sally was also surprised at the extent that Joey was sharing his understanding with others. She wondered if it was possible that Joey would come to speak to a group at her house.

So she said, "Joey, that's simply wonderful that you are speaking to so many. I see the great work you are doing and that you are preparing True Son to continue in your footsteps. I see that this is the work I have wanted to do all my life, but didn't know what to do or how to do it, until today when you said so clearly that everyone is Light and love. I am wondering if it is at all possible for you to meet with a small group of friends at my house to share with them what you have shared with us?" Again, Joey was floored--speak to a group of Whites? He had never thought of such a thing. "And," she said, "it would be delightful if Winnie and True Son could come too."

Roger hadn't expected this from Sally, though her spiritual side was continually exposing itself in their conversations. He was seeing more of Sally than he had seen before. There was a lot more to Sally than just what physically met his eye.

Joey thought and replied, "We'll have to talk about it. We have to see how we could fit it into our schedule. Could we call you later?"

Sally said, "Sure." So Sally gave them her phone number and directions, which wasn't far away.

Roger said, "We should be going. We've taken up a lot of your time and are really grateful to learn all that you have going on in your life. For myself, you've given me a lot to think about."

Sally agreed and said, "I'm so grateful. You have opened my mind and my heart. Thank you ever so much." Smiling goodbye and waving to True Son, they left.

Joey never had any idea what was going to happen next. Winnie was just as surprised as Joey. Again, they had another large issue to discuss and decide how they were going to handle this additional increase of activity in their lives..

Chapter 10

Into the White World

Speaking to a White group was something Joey had never considered--maybe one on one, but to a group? Thinking out loud he said to Winnie, "Suppose if I spoke to a White group this one time, do you think there's any possibility this could spread like it did through the reservations?"

Winnie replied, "Of course. There's a strong likelihood that it might. People share what excites them. Look how your words affected Sally. How many more White people are there who might be hungry like Sally? There's no telling how far this can go, and that gets a little scary. What if that happens, Joey? Are we prepared to handle that?"

Both were looking at the strong possibility that from one small group they might be up to their necks in requests to speak elsewhere. There was no way for them to know or predict what might happen. The White world was a huge place with great diversity in spiritual beliefs and pursuits. And knowing there was no one they could go to for guidance, they were just going to have to rely on their own inner judgments. So Joey said, "Let's let it rest, and maybe we'll get our answer if we both come up with the same feeling." They weren't into following intuitional knowing at that time, so their guidance was to go by feelings to determine the right choice they felt they should follow.

While they were letting the idea rest, the passing days saw the teen-agers discussing their developing understanding together, which, in turn, was forming a deeper feeling between them than had been their desire to drink together. They were becoming more and more interested in something outside of themselves which took them further out of their desire to drink. Their individual interest in life was returning, and that allowed them to feel the new energy others were feeling on the res. Their self-ostracized feelings toward their elders were disappearing, letting them associate more freely with them.

It didn't take long for them to begin asking how the fund raising was going for Joey's new house. They had walked by and had seen for themselves how tiny the ten-wide was that Joey's family lived in and saw their need to have a larger home. When they were told that a fund hadn't been started, they couldn't understand why? So they asked around when a fund was starting. They were interested because Charlie had asked them to help raise the money for a new home for Joey's family. Because they were teen-agers asking so many people the same question, they were causing quite a stir and that was triggering a need to have a meeting. The teen-agers had started something. They were eager about the fund and others could feel it. The time had come to have a meeting. The date and time was broadcast around by the teen-agers, but Charlie shouldn't know anything about it, because they felt it should be called Charlie's Fund, since it was his original idea.

That idea seemed to take hold--about 30 people turned out. They got down to business right away. All agreed that it should be called Charlie's Fund, which is why Charlie wasn't invited so that he couldn't veto the idea. And if Joey or Winnie asked about the fund, it could be said it was a project for the reservation and no one would be lying about it. One suggested that they open a savings account with the Credit Union that he belonged to, and that idea was accepted. Another suggested that it should be run by a committee. That was accepted as a good idea. Another suggested that it should be a committee of twelve and that all twelve signatures had to be on any withdrawal slip. That too was agreed upon. One of the teen-agers pulled a five dollar bill out of his wallet and said, "It's not much, but it's a beginning." They got over $150 to start the savings account. All donations from then on would be mail-in donations. One of the teen-agers gave his phone as the contact number for details to make donations. Little did he know how busy he was going to be.

Later, Charlie was informed of the meeting by the teen-agers. He was definitely surprised, but didn't like the use of his name. They explained to him all the reasons why it was called Charlie's Fund, and after he understood, he became agreeable with the idea. Silently he thought these kids are really smart. And so the little idea that Charlie had took off. Mike was one of those present at the meeting, and he told John about the fund at their next drumming. Good news gets around fast. Because of Charlie and the teen-ager's drinking issues that were no more, Charlie's Fund was good news, and before long the fund started growing.

While Charlie's Fund was being set up, Joey and Winnie had put their heads together, and they both came up with the same feeling.

The message of everyone being Light and love was not a message that could be confined to any one group of people, so in their feelings they both felt deeply they could not deprive anyone of hearing words that perhaps their soul had been deprived of hearing for a long time. White people with all their getting and accumulating material things for such a long time, have been under a tremendous strain of needing to achieve what society had told them their goals should be. Materialism was all around them. Commercialism continually pounded its message to buy, buy, buy all the allurements to feed the economy that wouldn't work if nobody bought anything. White people living their culture of materialism had produced a society of up-tight, stress-bound people of never having enough. Souls have been crying out for a long time for changes for the better.

Whether Joey or Winnie sensed all this was hard to fathom. They were just becoming more deeply aware of the White Man's world. Winnie had been living her peaceful way of life ever since she could remember. Joey's sharing of his Light experience with her had brought her the understanding of what she was already Being. So it was easy for both of them to see how lives in the White world would benefit by hearing what Joey had to share with them. What Winnie was not too keen on, was taking True Son into a situation of new people where neither she nor Joey had any idea of what to expect. Joey, although he would like to have Winnie and True with him, felt it not wise to do so. It was already feeling like it was going to be a big, new, unknowing experience for him. He felt that to have them with him would add considerably to his own strained feeling. When they discussed it, their same decision was no big surprise to either of them.

At the appointed date and time that he and Sally had agreed upon, Joey found himself in a residential neighborhood of neither old nor new houses. He saw Sally's house number and pulled up to the curb. He liked to arrive about a half hour before a meeting would start. He found it helped to feel being a part of the group which made him feel more at ease before beginning to speak. Before he got out of his truck, the voice in his head said, **"Relax, Joey, these are people just like yourself."** With those helpful words, he got out of his truck and walked up to the front door.

When he knocked, Roger opened the door and that further eased Joey's nervousness. Roger called Sally who dropped what she was doing, came and gave Joey a big hug. She had thought perhaps Winnie and their son wouldn't come--maybe a women's intuition was at work. But she was glad to see him and thanked him for coming. A few had already arrived and Joey was introduced to them. He and Roger never did get a chance to talk. People kept coming; altogether about 20 people showed up, which included an Indian friend whom Roger worked with and his Indian wife. Joey felt a little easier with three of his own race present. After all, this was his first experience of speaking to a White group. There were 3 or 4 men; all the rest were women. He had found that Sally had invited friends with whom she worked who, in turn, invited friends. Winnie was right. People are great advertisers when they're interested.

As people were getting comfortable sitting on the floor, Sally introduced Joey, telling about Joey's delightful wife and beautiful son, and said she was sorry they couldn't be here-- that they were all missing something in not meeting them. Joey thought how pleasant of Sally. Sally said, "I think we're all here to hear Joey tell his unusual spiritual story. Joey?"

Joey started by saying that this was the first time speaking to those who were not of his own race, and that if there were questions about Indian ways that weren't understood, to hold the questions until later and he would try to answer them. Then he started, "Winnie and I certainly didn't think anything spiritual was taking place when we first found our White son near the door of the church on our reservation. That thought never entered our heads. But let me back up a little and start from the beginning."

He felt that he had to tell about what they went through emotionally in losing their own son in stillbirth in order to get everyone on the same feeling page. Feelings were a big part of the story. He watched their faces as he told about their bald eagle sighting, how mystified they were and how it shifted their attention away from their loss, but he didn't detect anything. Then he told them about hearing a baby cry and then hearing it cry again and how they found a White baby in a basket next to the church door. He told how dumbfounded they were, and how they had no choice but to take the baby home with them and how, in just a short time they became very attached to this new little White addition. Then he told how they named him True Son so naturally. He didn't know whether he had made a connection with them or not. He did see that all eyes were glued on him, so he thought maybe he should ask at that point if anyone had any questions.

There was a question about what seeing the eagle meant. He answered, "In all tribes, because the bald eagle flies higher than any other bird and is very strong, it meant that to have an eagle sighting where it seems to be personal to the one seeing it, the eagle is considered a carrier of a good message from Great Spirit or God, as you call our Creator. We couldn't deny that our eagle sighting wasn't specifically for us, because it flew only about 30 feet above our heads in a tight circle three times. We had never talked about our cultural ways very much because we knew hardly anything about our ways. So the eagle made a strong impact on us. Now with our eagle sighting being a significant part of our story, it has renewed a great interest in the cultural ways of all of the tribes that I've spoken to. Does that answer your question?" The lady shook her head yes.

Another lady asked, "How's your son doing?"

Joey replied with what one could see as a loving grin, "He's just about as delightful and as much fun as you can imagine. He's keeping us busy trying to catch up with him. He's on the go all the time. Winnie has her hands full, but she's having a good time doing it. We're both looking to the day when he'll be toilet trained, but we haven't started that yet. Any more questions before I go on?"

Joey looked around. "No more questions?" He hesitated, "This is a good point to go on."

He then told how concerned he had been because he and Winnie had been given this perfect little white bundle from heaven. They felt that he was going to need a special spiritual education, and he said, "I knew I wasn't spiritual. I was at a real loss how True was going get the education he would be needing. Today, I still don't feel I'm a spiritual person. Maybe that's because everyone is a spiritual person and doesn't really know it. So when True Son was about three weeks old, the question about providing him with the right education was at the top of my mind, for I felt I was going to have to do some studying. I was walking home from work and....." He told them about kicking the rock which brought on the engulfing light and love experience he had. He went into detail describing the whole experience of the immense light and the great love that he had and how deeply he had been affected and how the light that completely engulfed him was the Light of his own soul. He told them about being that love and how everything in his vision and in his mind was that same love.

He finished by saying, "I still find it difficult to explain fully what that experience was completely like. There just aren't words that convey the immensity of that experience." He had gained a lot of experience in speaking to the many tribes about his experience, so he was able to tell it easily and in such a matter of fact, natural way that it left those hearing it kind of spellbound. No one moved. He said, "I know what I've just told you is way off your charts. So why don't we take a little break, have some of the nice snacks Sally has prepared and then we'll have fun with the questions." Sally spoke up and said, "Joey has been kind to share with us this evening. It would be nice if we said thanks with our hearts with an offering for him. We can pass this bowl around before we eat." It turned out to be a generous donation, a good sign that people appreciated hearing his message.

When they had all assembled again, Sally asked the first question. "Since we visited you at your home, I have been wondering about the light you were in and that everything was light, how that was the Light of your soul that you were seeing?"

Joey said, "It was told to me that I was actually seeing the Light of my own soul by three Elders who appeared in my Light experience. Their words were said inside my head and not outside of me which made their words all the more real. They were brighter than the rest of the light I was seeing. I've told this to very few, because I've felt the need to keep it to myself along with some instructional things that I also feel a need to keep to myself. Just how and what are the full mechanics of how this light appeared and that I was a natural part of it, is a big mystery to me. When I lifted my arm up to shield my eyes from the brilliant Light and I saw right through my arm, it was surprising beyond belief. I, as a soul, was at that moment seeing way beyond my normal vision. If I knew more than this I would share it with you. It only tells me that we are far greater than we will ever know if we continue thinking we are just a self. The full answer to your question, I believe, lies to be unveiled to all of us in future light experiences. We all have a beautiful destiny in experiencing the Light and love that we are." Sally seemed satisfied.

A lady's hand went up. She asked Joey about Light and love being the same thing, and could he say a little more about the great love that he mentioned?

Joey smiled and replied, "Sally asked a deep question and now you have asked another deep question. I'm smiling because I don't really have an answer. I've often wondered the same thing. All I really feel is that the inner love that flows out from our heart is of such a high nature that it possibly vibrates as light. When you feel this love it is at least a thousand times greater than any known love we have for each other, or for anything we've ever known."

This love cannot be controlled by our minds. We have to allow it flow forth freely from our hearts. It is complete in itself and needs no help from any thoughts we might have. It seems to act on its own wisdom and knows the life that it is. We are endowed with this love, but we have to learn to be the love that we are. Feeling-wise, because this love feels so beautiful, its high vibration might possibly cause it to be light. This is just a guess, mind you; it's just a guess. But there's absolutely no question that we are Light and great love. The Elders that I saw were great Light--great Light. I wish I could tell you more." Joey looked around and asked, "Does anyone else have a question that I can't answer?" And his smiling was joined by everyone else smiling with him.

A man asked, "Where will you be speaking next?"

Joey answered, "I will be speaking at a reservation about 100 miles from here next week. Why do you ask? "

"Oh," he said, "I thought you might be speaking close by. I'd like to hear you again."

Joey thought, here it comes. Joey said helpfully, "What you can do is get where it's quiet and think about being the Light and love you are. It might be helpful if you close your eyes and let go of your thoughts and just wait and see what feelings or revealing might develop. You see, I could tell you a hundred times that you are Light and love, but your life is the Light and love that you are, therefore it must be revealed to you from within before you really know it. Does that make sense to you?" The man smiled nodding yes, because that was a new idea to him.

Joey asked, "Anybody else?" Seeing there were no more questions, he said, "Thanks for a great evening. It's been really enjoyable being here. Thank you, Sally, for inviting me."

On the way home, Joey thought it good that Winnie and True stayed home. Too many were confined to a small space which would not have been at all practical for True. Basically, it didn't seem like it is right to parade True around at any of the evening speaking events. And nobody came up to him about speaking somewhere else later on, so for the moment at least he and Winnie didn't have that to consider. He did enjoy the evening, though; it was a nice new experience. Not much different than speaking at the reservations. The same deep interest was there, and he realized that Whites were really no different spiritually than his own race. This gave him a broadened perspective that he didn't fully have before.

A new view of their lives crossed his mind. He and Winnie had just turned twenty; both of them were born on the same day. What were the odds of something like that happening? That made him look at their lives. So much had happened in the last year at their young age. As he viewed their lives from a higher perspective, it made him wonder how all this could actually happen. These thoughts he would share with Winnie. She at times had a wiser picture of everything.

This blank area of wondering automatically opened the door for the Elders to speak before he ever reached home. While he was waiting at a stoplight, the voice inside his head took him by surprise saying, **"You and WindSong made a soul contract before being born into your present lives to raise your son to be a spokesperson of truth in order for many to know their true selves. True Son remembers himself as a Spirit Being. As he grows be aware of all that he sees and all he does. Always encourage him and support**

him." Joey gulped in amazement. The light turned green. Joey pulled across the intersection quickly and at the first chance he pulled over to the side of the street where he could think about what he had just heard without having to deal with driving.

That he and Winnie had chosen to be spiritual partners before being born, pretty much took his breath away. He had never in all his life ever entertained thoughts on such a vast, high level. But it sure made a lot of sense. It satisfied all his questions why he and Winnie had such love for each other and why True Son was in their lives. It was also a big help to know more about True Son. He also thanked his Elders for being Johnny-on-the-spot, so to speak, with crucial information exactly when it was needed. He thought too how comforting it is to know that the Elders are always close, and he thanked them from the bottom of his heart. When he reached home, Winnie was still up waiting, wanting to hear how Joey's meeting went in the White world, for she felt the evening marked a big turn in their lives.

Joey told Winnie all about the meeting, how Whites had the same deep interest in learning more of their own spiritual nature, and how nobody had asked for another meeting. That was a relief to Winnie's ears, but she was sure there would be more requests for Joey to speak later. Then Joey told Winnie what the Elders had said. She was not really surprised at their having a soul contract to raise True Son. She then offered, "You know, honey, I've seen True seeing something I couldn't see, and he responded laughingly a number of times. I know babies have their innocence, but the instances I'm telling you about seemed deeper and more of something going on. It's made me question if True has inner vision?"

Chapter 11

Joey and Winnie's Mission

It was back-to-school time on the res and the five teens felt the need to complete their high school education. The one who had given his phone number as a contact person for information on where to donate to Charlie's Fund found that he had to pass that task on to somebody else, somebody who was home all the time. So he talked to Charlie about it, and Charlie did find a woman who was willing. Charlie talked to some on the committee about circulating the idea directly to the reservations about Charlie's Fund and was that an appropriate thing to do? Charlie had wondered how all the reservations would get the word about the idea of trying to buy Joey a new home. Did they need to have a meeting? Charlie decided to ask the member who set up the account at the Credit Union, how much was in Charlie's Fund? It turned out there was over $5000 already in the account. That was a big surprise! The committee decided to hold a meeting. At the meeting they all pretty much felt that without any solicitation, donations were coming in at such an unexpected manner that they would let what was happening continue on its own. What they had no way of seeing was the way the idea of the fund was being circulated--that of how Charlie and the teen-agers had lost their desire to drink. Their story carried a tender message of the heart which affected everyone--a big thing on reservations, something a mere paper solicitation could never carry.

One on the committee suggested there were a number of mobile home locations that were in their proximity. Maybe it might be a good idea to see what was available and the prices so they would know what they needed as a total figure.

Nobody on the committee could know the reverent feeling there was for Joey on all the reservations that he had spoken at, how willing people were ready to give back to Joey in appreciation for what he had given them. Joey had triggered many hearts to open to their Great Spirit Light and love possibilities. It was not just a shot in the arm that Joey had given them. His words were more like a new energizing life that resonated deeply within them. His words were helping them to see more deeply into their cultural ways. On the reservations this new life was phenomenal. Something very real had replaced the hope that was scarcely there.

One of the strong traits of Indian life is to give, which is why offerings are often made to the four directions of the Medicine Wheel with feelings of meaningful gratitude, feelings of giving back to Mother Earth for all that she provides. Indians just have a natural tendency to be grateful, which is why Charlie's Fund had grown so quickly. Indians enter easily into creative sharing. In time creative sharing would take hold for all on Earth, as it would be seen that to share creatively would bring abundance to everyone. When hearts are open, creativity flows forth freely. Open-hearted giving is totally free of restricted mental positioning. Indians know well the principle that giving is the having, for it opens the feeling world, which mental positioning of how much to give never can.

History has shown a number of heart warming stories where Indians have helped White settlers who have settled into their territories by supplying them with food to help them survive. It has been postulated that if the Indians had been completely at peace within themselves and with others of other tribes, the European settlers could not have made war upon the Indians, and a whole different history of the European settlement would have been written, because basically it takes two opposing sides to engage in fighting. It would have been seen by the Europeans that in true peace there is love, and love does not fight. The integration of cultures would have been different. How different it might have been can only be speculated, for the Whites would have settled amongst thirty million peaceful Indians where peace and love would have rubbed off on them. This has been speculation only, but it does present the idea of "what if?"

Joey would in time get other invitations to speak to White groups, but the impact on them would never be felt like it was being felt on the reservations. Individual Whites would feel Joey's words impact their hearts and minds, but the group consciousness was not present like it was and has been on reservations. So Joey's message to the White world was on an entirely different playing field.

Not long after the Elders last spoke to Joey, Joey told Winnie, "I'm going to take True for a little walk; maybe he'll tire so he'll be ready for his nap." True was exceptionally energetic that day, and the fresh, warm September air would do them both good. True was being true to form; he ran on ahead of his dad, delighting in the freedom to run. He fell down a couple of times when his feet couldn't keep up with his body weight that was ahead of his feet.

He whimpered, but was off running again. They hadn't gone a block when True tired and sat down on the ground. Joey caught up with True and picked him up, walked a little further, turned around and was backtracking when very suddenly a big, beautiful dog was alongside of him. The dog was not the size of a St Bernard, but it was big, and it was trying to jump up on Joey, almost knocking him down. Joey had to put True down because the dog was determined to lick Joey's face. And it succeeded. Joey was having a time trying to keep this beautiful dog away from him. He commanded it to stay, and it did for about 30 seconds. Joey was wondering where this big dog with such a beautiful red fur coat came from. He hadn't ever seen it in the neighborhood before. He looked around to see if an owner was anywhere near. When he looked back, in front of him was the dog licking True's face with True laughing delightedly, turning his face from side to side. Joey got to True, picked him up and started to walk briskly back home. The dog walked alongside of Joey, swishing his tail hard and brushing his weight heavily on Joey. Joey was looking at True's face to make sure he was all right, when suddenly the dog vanished. It seemed to disappear into thin air.

The dog was gone, and True started squirming, wanting to be put down. So he put True down, and True started running making noise when he fell again. This time he was laughing again delightfully just as before. The dog, now invisible, was apparently licking True's face again. Joey couldn't help but think the dog was invisible, and that True could either sense or he could see the big dog. For sure something was making him laugh uncontrollably. When he picked True up, the laughing immediately stopped. He couldn't help but notice True's arms were reaching out and down toward something. His arms continued to reach out for about the next 50 feet or so.

As Joey reached home, he could see True was falling asleep. He washed True's face and laid him down to sleep, then washed his own face, which made Winnie question why he had washed their faces? Joey told her the whole story, how big and beautiful the dog was, and asked if she had ever seen a dog of that description around the neighborhood? To which she shook her head no. The sudden appearance and the equally sudden disappearance of the dog gave them both great wonder. And True apparently being licked the second time by an invisible something, gave them all the more to wonder about. They agreed that True's reaching down with his arms outstretched, indicated he was seeing something Joey couldn't see. The Elders had just said to support True, for he hadn't forgotten his spiritual identity. Now they thought that they could possibly see what the Elders were talking about. This dog experience had opened their eyes to be more alert now that True was past one and would be in his fast-developing years.

Both of them were deeply grateful that the Elders were watching over them with their guidance. These realizations that were expanding their awareness into new dimensions of life, were making them feel more and more insignificant.

The more they became aware of other dimensional life, the smaller they personally felt, because they had no knowable reference to it. It was one thing to have invisible Light and love and Elders to interact in their lives, but with another whole new dimension added to their awareness, it was going to take some time to incorporate this expansion into their understanding. A huge unseen universe was revealing itself.

Joey wondered and wondered about the beautiful dog. With its coat of beautiful red fur which seemed like a cross between an Irish Setter and a Golden Retriever, how did that animal suddenly appear and disappear? He had heard of ghosts, but this was no ghost--it had licked True's face and his too. The dog had been so loving that it crossed Joey's mind at the time that he'd like to make it his dog, but their tiny place shut that idea out as quick as he thought of it. That dog would capture anyone's heart. It evidently really appealed to True's heart too. Joey was sure if True could talk he would have a lot to say about the dog.

Speaking at the reservations was becoming less and less frequent, which gave Joey more time to ponder his many questions. He had found that as he received understanding on one point, more questions would pop up. He was finding there was no end to spiritual life. In fact, he was beginning to see that the physical world wasn't really physical. It had the appearance of being physical, but at the same time it obeyed spiritual law or a spiritual impulse. To Joey it was all so simple.

Science for all its scientific conclusions had not yet explained how a gigantic oak tree can grow from just a small acorn. Science can name an acorn's physical properties, but it cannot say how it knows how to develop into a mighty tree. This, he could see, holds true for all of nature.

On two different occasions he felt a Oneness with all of nature. Both times he felt like he was a part of life which was present everywhere. This life of which he knew himself to be a part, was the Life Force that gave all physical things their cause for being physical. Those two experiences of Oneness thoroughly warmed his heart with a love for everything in a way that exceeded the beautiful physical splendor of nature itself, for the experience of the reality of nature's Oneness added grandeur to one's feeling that far exceeded what visual beauty alone can provide. He came to know how the forebears of his race felt when they lived so close to the land. They had great admiration and respect for the Great Spirit which lived in everything, thus their respective consideration for all life was always in the forefront of their minds. This made it natural for them to give thanks to Great Spirit before they took an animal's life or when they harvested their crops or took from nature her offerings for their welfare.

How different were the Indian ways of old compared to White man's ways of robbing the Earth of her resources, that carelessly left behind a huge blanketing trail of pollution. Obvious to almost everyone, and still is, is the lack of feeling in the White Man's ways of living an artificial life. Joey in his true seeing the current conditions everywhere, was seeing that the inner spiritual life must always govern the outer physical life. Without it, life becomes exceedingly barren, with huge resulting consequences . These thoughts played almost constantly before Joey's awareness, and more and more he felt like he had a mission in life, the whole of which he could not yet see clearly. Thus questions lingered in his mind.

One of the big questions that continually occupied the forefront of his mind was, in what direction is the whole of mankind headed? Is it headed toward oblivion or is there something on the horizon which would alter and change the direction of the future for mankind? Winnie wondered too. News media seldom reported on good news, so there was nothing hopeful or bright in the mainstream of media news. Yet to both of them--since they knew and felt Spirit to be so much in charge of everything, except, of course, the hearts and minds of people who have free will, their Creator had to be in charge of what was going to be the future for mankind. They felt sure there had to be an answer. If there wasn't any future for the better, why were they raising True Son? Surely there had to be a high spiritual purpose in the mind of the Creator that gives life to everything. In answer to their probing interest, Winnie suggested, "Maybe the Elders can give us the answer we're looking for."

Joey responded, "Yes. Hopefully they can tell us what we need to know, but we never know just when they will speak to us. They said to ask, and now we're asking." So they let it rest and began to do the household things that always needed doing.

The next day Winnie went shopping while Joey watched True. She wouldn't be gone long--True was asleep and Joey had to go to work soon. Winnie had only been gone five minutes when the Elders spoke audibly inside his head, "**We have heard your discussions, and we have wondered how long it would be before you would be asking the large question that is on your mind. Your question is all in good timing.**"

"**What you are seeing in your world is the birthing of a new day, a new time in our Creator's Great Cycle of Times. Your humanity, as a whole, is leaving the long age of separation and is entering a new time of unification where everyone will live the ways of their Creator. All people will become unified by the agent of love in their hearts. They will come to know that their nature is love like our Creator is love. Thus for each one their own love will lead the way, and love will bind all together as One in equality, in worth and in intelligence out of which even the history of separation will not be remembered. Do you have any questions?**"

Being allowed to ask questions was a first for Joey, so he was thoughtful for a time until he framed his question, "I fully sense what you have just said is true, although I had not pictured it that way. These times seem to be rough for everyone. How is everyone to get through these rough times to when it will be much better? There don't seem to be any bright spots out there."

"**The bright spot you speak of is in your own heart. Love is the bright spot you seek. You have taught about the love you have experienced, and you know its high value in your life. Everyone has this same high value, but that value waits to be uncovered by each one. The life of everyone can be rough with all of its ups and downs without the heart's love. The big shift to this new cycle will be the great change from living from the mind to that of living from the heart. Mind by itself sees only separation, whereas the heart knows only unity. When one lives from their** heart, rough times no longer exist, for one lives in the unity of peace, love and Light. Does that answer your question?"

"Yes, it does. It's all so very simple," Joey replied in thought. "Mind by itself surely does complicate everything when it thinks on its own." Joey asked mentally, "How long will this great change take?"

The Elders spoke again saying, **"Some will get the message quickly, for they will be receptive to the truth of it. For others, it will depend on how long it will take them to wake up; therefore, we cannot give you a definite time. But what you can rely on is that this new cycle is one of higher energy, which gives the change a great impetus to proceed according to our Creator's plan. Live in the only moment there is, which is right now and everything will be according to universal order. Everything functions in perfection accordingly. Our Creator holds each of us in Its sacred way. We need not worry about anything when we live Great Spirit's life."** With that Joey was left alone to contemplate all they had said. And then he thought he'd better write it all down before it left him.

Right after he finished writing, Winnie was back. When she came in, she saw Joey grinning, so she asked, "What are you so happy about?" Joey told her the Elders had just spoken to him, answering their big question, and that he had written down all they had said. She could study their words, but he had to go. He grabbed his lunch, kissed her heavily and was out the door. For the rest of that day and for many days following, Joey felt happier and lighter than he had for a long time. There was a bright future for everyone.

Winnie studied Joey's written words. She too felt greatly relieved when she understood the full picture. Everything fell into place nicely. Her mind became exceptionally clear, and intuitively she could see the Creator's great plan for His creation on earth. What once had been a great Light at the beginning of time became diminished when their original ancestors chose to experience a lesser light of their own mental thinking to live in. Now the Great Light of Spirit was returning to once again illumine the Earth and everyone upon it. She saw the new cycle vividly. Everything was lit by the Light of love. Her already happy heart became overjoyed with love. It was like the Elders had foretold; it was a new day and a new time. Silently with great joy she thanked the Elders for revealing such joyful words of truth. The truth of the Elders' words had found fertile soil in her heart, as it would also find fertile soil in the receptive hearts of many others.

CHAPTER 12

SPIRITUAL EXPANSION ON THE RESERVATION

WORD WAS GETTING AROUND THE res that the drumming group was having a good time during their drumming sessions in addition to experiencing an increased sense of well-being. That was sparking curiosity in others to attend the meetings. Mike began to feel that something more was needed in the drumming gatherings to make the meetings more spiritually beneficial. He wondered if he could get Joey to attend. He thought if he approached Joey at work, it might seem a more casual way of asking him.

Mike thought about it for a few days and decided to act. Mike drove by Joey's home to see if his truck was gone, which it was, so he continued on to Don's Auto Service. He pulled in to a pump and went inside to pay for gas and found Joey cashiering. Greetings were made, and he said to Joey casually, "You know, we're having a lot of light-hearted fun drumming and our numbers are growing. We'd like you to be there too. You would add a lot to our group with all your wisdom. If you don't have a drum, I'll see to it that you get one. I think you'd enjoy relaxing and having fun with the rest of us. What do ya say?"

Without much thinking, Joey said, "Yeah, I'd like to give it a try"

Mike thanked him saying, "Great. I'll see to it that you'll have a drum" and left to fill up his tank. Joey wondered afterward why he said he would attend so quickly. His reply was really out of his mouth before he had considered the idea.

Mike got a hold of John right away, and John learning the drum he was requesting was for Joey, said, "This drum will be on us, Mike. It'll be our joy to give Joey a drum covered with elk skin so that it will have a deep, resonant voice. Are you still meeting on the second Tuesday of the month?" To which Mike said that they were. John said, "Good. We'd like to be there to give it to him. Okay?"

Mike said, "Great, and thanks ever so much, John. I know everyone will appreciate your gift to Joey in addition to Joey's great surprise and gratitude." Mike called Joey right away to let him know that John would be at the next drumming and that John would add a lot to the session.

The weeks went by quickly, during which time Joey thought more and more about drumming. He shared with Winnie that he never had any desire to drum. He didn't know why. There just hadn't been any compulsion to want to drum. Whether the love he felt in his heart was totally satisfying, he couldn't really say. All he knew was that he was going to a drumming because he had been invited. Winnie's only comment was, "Don't try to figure it all out, just go and have fun. Leave the rest to Spirit." Joey had to agree. He was glad that Winnie was always so practical, so right on target with just the right words. To him, she is an amazing person for whom he is continually grateful for the great love she is in his life. It worked both ways. In their love, they were always there for each other.

Others were arriving at the same time Joey arrived, and the happy moments began. Mike greeted Joey with grateful words for his coming. Joey was shown where the coffee was, and pretty soon almost everyone had arrived including John and his friends. Greetings were exchanged, and a single drum beat was heard signaling everyone to get situated to begin. Mike began by saying how grateful he was that Joey and John and his friends could come.

He asked John if he wanted to say something?

John said it was good to be with old friends again. Then he addressed Joey, saying that it was a deep pleasure to see him again, something Joey didn't expect, and Joey acknowledged the feeling was mutual. Then John said, "Joey, we learned that you didn't own a drum, so we felt it would honor our tribe if you would accept this drum we made for you?" And then John pulled a beautiful new drum out of a special leather carrying case. He got up and presented it to Joey. Joey was dumbfounded. He stammered out a thank you as best he could. John asked, "Will you hold it up for a minute, Joey?" which he did. Then John began praying in his native tongue to Great Spirit to bless the drum. There were a couple of moments of deep reverence that everyone could feel, because of the sincerity in which the drum had been given.

Joey was really taken by surprise, and again tried as best he could to say thank you. It seemed everyone in the room liked Joey's new gift as much as Joey did. The feeling in the room was exemplary; it was hard to define. There was a lot of conversation going on amongst everyone. Mike, after a few moments, asked Joey if he would open with a prayer to get them all focused. Joey was surprised. He hadn't expected this, but he nodded okay.

He started by saying, "To be honest, I really don't know how to pray--I never do. I just talk to Great Spirit like the Spirit is always around me, which I know It is. So, I'll just say Thank you, Great Spirit, for working with everyone who has had a part in making this beautiful drum for me. It's a wonderful gift that I deeply treasure. And I thank you for being present with everyone here. Shower each one with the blessing they need." And laughing he said, "and help me learn to drum."

Most in the group were somewhat surprised at the manner in which Joey addressed Great Spirit, like It was a person he was talking to, but the natural sincerity in Joey's voice and choice of words made it all very real and a little humor added to the naturalness. Mike asked John if he would lead the group, to which John said he'd be happy to. John noticed that the group had grown more together since he was last there, and he praised them. John said after a few songs, "Let's just drum without singing, so Joey can join with our beat. I will change the beat from time to time. Okay?"

So Joey soon found the rhythmic beat having an effect in his feeling world. He liked it. After a time, he found the unison in the drum beat entrancing. The steadiness of the beat altered his mental state somewhat, to where he had a deeper awareness of everything and everyone being One. When John went to a different beat, he lost his awareness. He had to use his mind to adjust to the different tempo. He was totally surprised to have felt completely One with everyone. Oneness he thought was one of the greatest feelings that one can have. Now he realized how the drum had become a revered unifying instrument. What he did not know at the moment was the significant role the drum played in the many indigenous cultures throughout the world.

In very short order, Joey learned the spiritual effects of drumming that sometimes takes a long period of time for others to have the same experience, but he had no way of knowing that. He liked the singing too, voices singing as One, though he couldn't remember much of anything later. It proved to be a really fun evening in many ways. It was a relaxing time. He was glad that he hadn't been asked to say something. No sooner had the thought crossed his mind when Mike asked, "Did you enjoy the drumming, Joey?"

Joey answered he did and added almost without thinking, "I enjoyed being in a state of Oneness with everyone here."

Mike looked at Joey keenly, "I don't understand you. What exactly do you mean by being One with everyone here?"

Joey then asked, "Doesn't everyone feel Oneness when they drum?"

Everyone looked at each other questioningly. Mike said, "Well, I've never had the experience you've described." Has anyone else had a Oneness experience like Joey has described?"

John answered, "We drum because we feel like we're closer to Great Spirit's heartbeat. I think we all feel we'd like to feel what you've felt, Joey. How did this happen?"

Joey said, "Well, I guess the steady drumming beat kind of made me let go of my thoughts. I just seemed to be more aware, at that point is when I felt like we were all One."

Mike asked, "What do you mean, you let go of your thoughts?"

"I think a lot less these days than I did a year ago," Joey explained, "I guess mostly because I realized that the thoughts that were continually running through my mind weren't doing me any good at all. Once I saw the way I was thinking, I didn't want to think like that anymore, so I pretty much stopped thinking, and I started to be more peaceful in my mind and much more aware of what was going on around me. Maybe that's why I slipped so easily into feeling the drumbeat and entered into being One with everyone here. Feeling being One with everyone is one of nicest feelings I have felt in my whole life. I really feel this is what our ancestors felt when they would sit around campfires and drum. It was a big part of their life."

John offered, "I know what you've said is true. I remember when I was young and used to drum with the elders, they would get deep smiles on their faces like something was happening within them. Being young, I never paid too much attention to them and never gave it much thought. But you've really refreshed my memory tonight. I feel like I've really learned something. Thank you." Many were nodding their heads in agreement. Their interest had been really kindled.

Mike said, "I've got a few years on me, but I'm never too old to learn. Joey, do you think you could come again and talk more about how we can let go of our thoughts?"

Joey's new mission came to mind which caused him to reply in the affirmative. Besides, he would like to drum again. John asked if he and his friends could come again too.

Everyone chimed in, "Of course, you can come anytime."

Before John left, Joey got to thank John again saying, "The drum has a nice deep sound to it."

John replied, "Yes, it's elk skin, heavier and more resonant than deer skin. It's on an 18" cedar frame that deepens its voice. One of the women made the leather carrying case. She said that a good drum needs a good case."

Joey said, "It's very beautiful. Be sure to tell her I said thanks and give her a big hug."

John said, "I will. She's my wife."

Joey said goodnight to everyone as soon as he could. He wanted to get home to show Winnie his new drum, and when he did, he was feeling like a little kid with a new toy. In his happiness, it seemed he couldn't get the words out fast enough, telling about how the drumming session went. When he told her about what the next meeting was going to be like, she was happy for him, for she had wondered when the tribe was going to ask more of Joey. He had gained so much understanding in a year that it was just obvious that he could help his neighbors, perhaps in a deeper way. It seemed that Winnie's perception of their future activities was always right on the mark.

Word seemed to get around the reservation fast. Interest was kindling for the residents to learn more of their spiritual nature. It wasn't that the revelation of everyone's Being is Light and love was wearing off, it was the need to learn how to access and experience their own Light and love. Their interest had been whetted to learn more. Was it possible to get Joey to tell them more about what he felt they needed to know at the get-together? Eventually the question was put to Charlie, for he was more or less in charge of the potlucks.

Charlie thought it was a good idea, since Joey and Winnie were attending anyway. He would frame the request like it was almost imperative that those on the res were very hungry to be fed spiritually. When he told Joey how everyone was needing more of the good medicine he had to share, his mission came to mind automatically, and he said he would. Joey could see now that he was going to be much busier than he thought. He also saw that he was going to need to present information in a joyful way, otherwise the truth that he wanted to share would not take hold. He didn't see much point in trying to share spiritual ideas if they weren't uplifting. When he shared his concern with Winnie, again she said, "Just be yourself."

Joey wasn't too surprised that several had brought tape recorders to the get-together. He thought it was a good idea. When Joey got up to speak, True Son who had been somewhat fidgety, began crying when his dad left him. Winnie tried to soothe him, but he kept on crying--he wanted his dad. So Joey had to go back and take him in his arms. Joey tried to tell True that it was okay to be with mommy, but True wanted to stay with his daddy. So Joey had no choice but to talk with True in his arms. By this time all felt that this was really one big family affair. It put a homey touch on the evening.

Joey began by saying, "I'm glad to see some tape recorders here. If my words prove to be helpful, there can be some reference to them later. I want to ask you, are you Indian?" Everyone nodded and murmured yes. Joey said, "That's funny, I thought you were Light and love," to which there was more murmuring. "Well, which is it? Are you Indian or are you Light and love?" Now some didn't like the spot he was putting them on. Indians have a deep reverence for their race and culture. Joey got their attention right away. "Does anyone have something to say?" He waited and no one spoke up.

He continued, "I can see I struck the right nerve, for I wanted you to recognize how deeply you hold your personal treasures. These very strong ideals which truly have their right place in our lives, are really what prevent any one of us from experiencing the Light that we are. What we hold in our minds blocks the Light from being our experience. When we hold these deep thoughts and their resulting feelings above Great Spirit being the highest and most important thing in our lives, we do a great dishonor to ourselves. Because we are Great Spirit living on Earth, we can in no way ever think that we can ever hold a greater idea than being Great Spirit, regardless of what we may think. Now this goes for all other nationalities and all other cultures as well, for all must bow in mind and heart to the One Great Spirit-Source that we are. Are you with me on this?" Everybody understood what Joey was driving at.

Joey said, "Let's take this a bit further, shall we? What if we go around continually thinking thoughts all the time? Does that give an opening for the Great Spirit which we are, a chance to speak to us?" There was silence. Nobody was stirring--not even True. Joey said, "We have a mind, but we are not our mind. We use the One Spirit Mind to think thoughts, and we have a heart out of which flows a beautiful love which is life itself. Life lived from the open heart that is always loving everyone and everything, is the epitome of living life. Because only the heart knows life in the same manner that Great Spirit knows life, the mind can then create thoughts that are in synch with Great Spirit life. When the mind creates thoughts on its own, it creates thoughts in an endless fashion that does not allow the heart's love to flow outward. Does everyone understand that?"

Someone asked, "You don't mean the physical heart, do you?"

"No. The heart I'm speaking of isn't physical," Joey replied, "It's the center of your Being. It's the center where your love comes from, like when you love a child or spouse, a little puppy or playful kitten. You can't locate it physically, but you can feel it. The greater the love that pours out of your heart, the greater the feeling. The feeling of Great-Spirit-love is utterly sublime. There is no equal to it."

Then he went on to tell them what the Elders had said about Earth entering a new cycle of time that is the Creator's high plan, of how everyone will change from living in their heads through thinking thoughts to living the love that flows from their hearts. "This," he said, "is the future for everyone on Earth. This is what I feel some of our ancestors knew, but which has been mainly forgotten. In time we will have the extreme pleasure of living a life that exceeds anything the Red race has ever known. Everyone will know the love that they are, and light will shine on everything that everyone does. This is the Creator's plan for everyone."

True was falling asleep, so while they were thinking about what he had just said, he walked to where Winnie was and gave True to her open arms. He asked again if there were any questions. Several hands shot up. They all basically had the same question. They wanted to know how such a change could take place when there seemed to be no end to the wars that continually sprouted up, and also there appeared no solution to the ever expanding financial problems that made living so precarious. With so much chaos everywhere, to them, there seemed no solution. The idea of a better life didn't compute with what was happening in the world.

Joey was sure this ultra-large question was sure to pop up. So he began by saying, "We all want to see bright spots in the outer world which assures us that changes for the better are correcting the problems. The Elders have said the bright spot we're looking for is Great Spirit's love that is in our own heart. As each of us finds that Great-Spirit-love in our heart, that love will brighten the world with its light. This is why love is really the savior in our day and time. Everyone is love--that's who everyone really is.

"It's all so simple. Our Creator is love and out of love our Creator created Beings like unto Itself who are also love. You can never be anything other than the love that created you, even if you consider yourself to be something other than love. Think of it this way. When you refer to yourself as I someone or something, whatever that might be, think of the I of yourself to be love instead. It's a beautiful change to the true identity of who you really are. When you say I am this or I am that, you really are the Great Spirit that thinks it is something else. This is the big illusion we all face. This universal message is being spread throughout the world by many others, not just to this tribe alone.

"This is why we must be very aware of what we think. When we are aware and watching our thoughts, we will recognize if our thoughts are really being useful, or if they are just rampant thoughts running through our mind that have no meaning or usefulness in our lives. Once we have seen the thoughts that continually cross our minds, we can easily let go of all that is no longer helpful. In time we will have a peaceful mind through which the heart opens to radiate its love.

"Your thoughts determine your world. How you see life and how you perceive the world is what you believe, and you live your life according to what you believe. You believe what you think because your thoughts are your creations. People strongly defend their creations, which is why people have so many disputes with each other. We are all the one common denominator of One Spirit. When people learn this, we will all be on the same page. We will all have the same understanding, same interests and the same goals. We will know and live as a whole to bring about the best for everyone. This is what the new cycle is all about. I don't have to worry about what you do, and you don't have to concern yourself with what I do. We all have our own inner work to do. That's enough for anyone. When we follow our own personal inner pathway, we lose all interest in criticizing or judging others, because as our hearts open up to let Great-Spirit-love be our life, that beautiful love never sees another's weaknesses. Great-Spirit-love knows only love for everything."

Joey was feeling a gushing joy as he said, "I wish I could tell you what a beautiful Being each of you are. You are a Light that wants to expand, and you are the love that knows no end. Everyone walks in a place of great peace. That peace is found by eliminating all those thoughts that have no relevance to your well-being.

"We live in a great period of time. This old age of many troubles is dying out and a new age of heaven on Earth is beginning. We are seeing old ways crumble, because those ways do not serve everyone, because there is no love activity in them. The old parasitical way of everyone making a profit off everyone else will die out. We are entering a time of creative sharing that will be beneficial to everyone. We Indians have this way of creative sharing deep within our hearts already, and it is just waiting to blossom forth. Our Creator's light is shining upon us, making our pathway ahead clear and bright. Does anyone have anything to say or add to what I've just said?" That was the essence of his message for the evening.

There were a few more questions, with Joey responding to each one.

There were lots of personal thanks as they departed. Winnie said on the way home, "I think you said it all very well. Everyone was left with a lot to think about. True wanting to be with you turned out to be an asset. Everybody could identify with the three of us and could feel us being a part of the bigger family," and she said, "I'll bet you're tired, so I'll put True to bed." They were home and Joey knew that the big ideas that he shared, would have to have time to incubate, because he knew that the bigger picture he was seeing for humanity, was still perking in his own mind.

It turned out that small groups gathered together to listen to what Joey had said and to discuss the ideas he shared. He had been effective in opening their minds to consider the larger ideas of what affects their lives.

CHAPTER 13

JOEY LEARNS THE GREAT WHITE SHAMAN'S WISDOM

A COUPLE OF DAYS HAD GONE by since the get-together, and Joey began to feel like there was something more he should know. This feeling kept getting stronger and stronger as each day passed, until he found himself wondering what it was that had grabbed a hold of him to the point where he could not entertain any other thought. What was it that he needed to know? He had examined his understanding of all that he knew spiritually, but found nothing he felt that needed to be enlarged upon, so he kind of gave up. At that restful point in his mind, the Elders had his full attention.

It surprised him when they spoke, saying audibly in his head, **"Joey, the time has come when you need to broaden your scope of knowing to include the understanding of what the Great White Shaman taught 2000 years ago. This can best be done by talking with the White minister on your reservation. You will need this understanding in the times ahead."** Joey never could have guessed that studying Jesus' words was the answer to his wondering. He shared with Winnie what had occupied his attention for the past several days and what the Elders had advised him to do.

Winnie acknowledged that she knew something was spinning around in his mind, but thought it best not to pry. She asked him what he was going to do, to which he replied, "Well, I guess I'll be contacting Ron. The Elders said I should, and that makes sense. I know he's been doing a lot of studying for several months now, so he should be a big help."

To say that Ron was overjoyed when Joey asked him to help him understand what Jesus taught, was an understatement. Ron was more than delighted, for he really needed someone like Joey who could really see into some of Jesus' words that he could not yet fully understand. So, to Ron, it was going to be a time of equal sharing, but at the same time, he thought he would gain more than Joey would.

They arranged a time that was suitable to both, and when they met, Ron began by saying, "I bought you this King James version of the Bible that has Jesus' words in red so that we don't have to bother reading the narrations. I've been wanting to get as close as possible to what has been handed down as His teachings. As there have been many, many persons who have copied and translated the various manuscripts over the centuries, there is no telling how far the texts are from their original source. And too, all that makes up the New Testament was written many years after Christ's crucifixion and resurrection. The King James Version was translated from a number of Greek manuscripts that were scattered around Europe in the early seventeenth century. It is felt that these Greek manuscripts had been translated from the original Aramaic. Nobody knows for sure. But what we do know is that there are a number of translations of the Bible from the King James Version, which have lost a lot of the meanings that are retained in the King James Version. To me, translations made from an original translation from the Greek, are about as close as we can get to what Jesus said. Translators are very apt to reduce His words according to their own beliefs. I don't feel they have done this intentionally. It's just natural that a person or a group of people would do this, because people do not like to swim in water that's way over their heads when it comes to their understanding. I can show you, if you'd like, where meanings have been lost in the translation of His words in other versions when compared with the King James Version?"

Joey certainly had no idea about the Bible. He just thought the Bible was the Bible. But answering Ron, he said, "I think I can see where you have done the right kind of research, and I know that you're looking for the truth in the words that Jesus said that points you to the truth within yourself, so if we bump into those differences as we go along, that's fine. There's no need to point them out now. And thank you ever so much for this Bible. I never intended for you to do anything like that."

Ron said, "It's my pleasure. You've opened up a whole new world of spiritual understanding for me and I'm very grateful."

Joey said, "Since I don't have much time today, is there something you'd like to point out to me now that you think would be helpful?"

Ron answered, "I really don't know what it is that would be most helpful to you right now. But when you read over His words, you will gain a larger picture of His teachings which we can talk about at a later time. If I'm seeing this correctly, I think the Elders want you to know about this great man on your own, and I think your own intuition will help you understand the depth of His meanings. If and when you go out into the White world where the Bible is the prominent teaching book, you will be fortified with the understanding that will be most helpful in that world. We know that the teachings the Master taught and the teachings of the Great Spirit are all one truth, but the majority have no idea of truth at all. I say that because I was raised in the White world where everything spiritual is outside of them. There is very little looking inward. When we look inward, we find there is a lot to learn about ourselves."

Joey said, "Amen. By the way, how do you think the last get-together went?"

"Well, you gave us a lot to think about. In a way I think it was equal to your first sharing about everyone being Light and love. These big ideas are much bigger than our common ordinary lives, so it takes a while to accept them and to digest them. I know, because I speak for myself. I'm still trying to absorb the great implications that your message of what a whole new cycle of time implies. You really did stretch our imaginations way beyond where we normally are."

Joey said, "Yes, I know. The Elders stretched me too. We're all in the same boat. But when we look at it all in the right perspective, it's the only thing that makes sense. It gives us that far-reaching vision we all need for the times we're in. The beauty of it is that it is truth from On High of Great Spirit." Ron nodded in agreement.

Joey said as he was leaving, "Thanks again for the Bible and the lesson on its origin. I believe it would have taken me a long time to learn what you have shared with me. I will read Jesus' words, and I will let you know when we need to get together again. Many, many thanks, Ron."

Ron echoed, "Goodbye--see you later."

When he got home, Joey showed Winnie the nice Bible Ron gave him and told her why it was Ron's choice of many versions. Winnie confessed she knew nothing about the Bible but was glad that Ron did. It seemed to Winnie that the Bible was a lot more complicated than the love and Light of Great Spirit. Jokingly she said to Joey, "I'm sure glad you got the direction to study the Bible and not me."

Joey replied also in jest, "Don't be too sure of yourself, honey. In time you might find yourself reading it to satisfy your curiosity. Who knows what lies ahead for any one of us? Who knows what we are going to expand into knowing? We are infinite are we not?"

Winnie nodded, "You got me."

The drumming session was coming up in about two weeks. They were having breakfast when he mentioned to Winnie wondering, "Do you suppose there will be more attending the drumming meeting because of what I shared at the get-together?"

Winnie, after swallowing what she was chewing on, replied, "Quite possibly. Mother told me that small groups have been meeting to hear the tapes again which have stirred up big questions in peoples' minds. There just might be more people there than there were last time."

Joey said that was what he was seeing too. "Also, there's a keen interest in those who were there about what their thoughts had to do with how effective their drumming efforts were."

Winnie said, "True. That's what triggered a bigger attendance at the get-together."

Joey was silently wondering if he had all the answers to the many questions that might be asked. At that point the Elders spoke, saying audibly inside his head for the first time in the presence of Winnie,

"Joey, just read the words of the Great White Shaman."

When he told Winnie what the Elders had just said to him, she asked how he heard the Elders, to which he answered, "I just hear a voice inside my head which sounds just like hearing a voice outside myself. I also feel a higher or quicker vibration in my body as the

Elders speak. It's kind of like I know when it's them speaking. It's one voice speaking for all three of them. It's always a good feeling."

Winnie felt Joey's good feelings and was satisfied. She wondered why she hadn't asked that question sooner, for his answer made her feel a deeper connection with the Elders and caused her to think how wonderful to be so closely connected with what she felt was a heavenly Source. Evidently Winnie's own high awareness allowed her to feel what Joey feels when the Elders speak to him. It made her smile deeply within.

Joey had some time before needing to leave for work. So he settled down comfortably with his new Bible and opened it at the beginning. His eyes fell upon the words that described the history of how the King James Version came to be. Interesting he thought. Pretty much just as Ron had described but with a more complete history. Then he turned to the New Testament.

Joey was very glad that Ron had chosen a Bible that had Jesus' words printed in red. All the words in the whole of the four gospels seemed overwhelming to Joey, for he had never been much for reading more than was necessary at any given time. So reading/ studying was trying for him. He was glad to find that as he read Jesus' words, they were very simple, and as he was to read further, he found His simple words to be very profound, like saying to a large gathering on a hillside in the Gospel of Matthew, "Love your enemies, and pray for those who persecute you;" so simple a statement, but so big on emphasizing the value of love.

Joey found that he liked what he was reading, was almost without effort. Jesus' words were resonating deeply within him. In a very short period of reading, he was finding a kinship with Jesus. It was a kinship of brotherhood, similar to tribal kinship, but much stronger and much deeper in feeling. It was a kinship of purity. What he was feeling was surprising to him. He had never felt like this before. He had no idea that such feeling existed. He looked at the clock; it was time to go to work. He wanted to read more, but he had to go. Not saying anything to Winnie about his feeling, he grabbed his lunch, kissed her goodbye and left. For the rest of his workday he continued to feel a connection of brotherhood with Jesus. Jesus' words had a profound effect upon him. Later, he read all His words in the four gospels and continued to be amazed at the truths stated so simply.

The Elders had been correct in calling Jesus a great Shaman. From what he had read, Jesus had kind words for everyone, except the church rulers. He healed many and taught the way to live a happy life. He thought to himself that the Whites who took the land away from his race, surely didn't live what He taught. And he also saw that it was obvious that those who were running the national government, didn't live His teachings either. What a sad picture. People have a way to live a happy life and don't live His teachings. They seem to be oblivious to what He taught.

When he and Ron got together again to discuss Jesus' teachings, Ron explained to Joey in the best way he knew why people didn't live according to the only right way to live if they wanted to have a happy life. He thought people wanted the things of the world more than they wanted a happy life. Joey would later learn there was more than one reason that people were so engulfed in the darkness of their own mind. Basically, now that Joey had read and to some degree studied Jesus' teachings, both of them felt Jesus was a great teacher in many respects. Joey could now identify with those on the res who went steadily to hear Ron's message about Jesus and how Jesus influenced their lives. Studying Jesus' teachings gave Joey a tremendously enlarged perspective of where White people were at in how they viewed life. This better understanding of White people made him feel more connected to their race. The "them" of the White people seemed to disappear in his new feeling of their being love and Light. His heart had the same sadness for them as he held for those of his own race who did not know their Great Spirit Source.

He was grateful to his Elders for urging him to study Jesus' teachings. His consciousness had become more inclusive of the land he lived in. It certainly was good to have this wider perspective. It made him feel more connected to people as a whole, and in time he would no longer see people having different colored skin.

The drumming session would be taking place in about two weeks, and he was looking forward to it.

The nights were noticeably longer, with the daytime shadows growing longer too. Fall weather always held a kind of nostalgia which felt natural to him. He never questioned this feeling that he always felt in the fall, but now he began to wonder why it was so prevalent with him.

At this time he felt like he wanted to learn more about his own Spirit nature. He began to feel like he should find time to get still within himself. How he would do that in their small place, he didn't know. So he asked Ron if it was okay if he could use the church in which to get quiet. Ron said, "Absolutely. That's what it's for."

He talked to Winnie about his feeling of needing to get quiet. "Of course," she said, "I often have the moments to do that. It really refreshes me; always it leaves me to enjoy what I'm doing in a fuller way." Again Joey thought Winnie to be a wonderful spiritual person. Her thoughts dove-tailed again with his own. He thought how wonderful can it get?

Much to Joey's surprise, his initial attempts to still his mind didn't result in his mind getting still at all. His mind was too agitated. Then he thought, I'll just watch my thoughts as they appear before me, and as he did he found that he relaxed. He had built up tensions by trying too hard. He saw that as he relaxed more and more, his mind actually slowed down--his thoughts became less and less, and he began to feel a more wholesome feeling throughout his whole body, not a tingling exactly, but more like a quickening vibration. From then on, his mind did become still, and there was a heightened feeling of being more centered within.

He didn't actually think it, but for a person going on 21, he was experiencing very quick results in meditation. He found that as soon as his mind stopped thinking, his heart opened wide to experience the pure love of his Creator which, in turn, gave him a feeling of Beingness that he had never experienced before. It was wonderful, thrilling and completely satisfying. It was peace, love and joy fullness all at once. There were no words that could do Beingness justice. He was home. He felt more than a replenishment. It gave his mind an aliveness and alertness or awareness that was much keener than ever before. He was finding his Spirit nature to be a lot more than just the physical body or his mind. It was kind of like a deliciousness that he felt throughout his body that descriptively was beyond any feeling he had ever experienced.

Joey was a high soul when he came into his present incarnation which is why many wonderful spiritual experiences were coming to him at such an early age. But of course he knew nothing of this.

CHAPTER 14

THE DRUMMING LESSON

LUCKILY JOEY HAD A GOOD boss. Don accommodated Joey's work schedule so that the days when he was to speak to a gathering, he worked the first shift, got off early or had the day off. Don didn't know why, but he felt kind of fatherly toward Joey. And because Joey was very conscientious in everything he did, there was a strong mutual feeling of good will for each other.

Joey thought of the drumming session that evening and how fortunate he was to have what to him was a good job and to be working for a good boss who made it possible for him to speak when he needed to. Joey didn't know it, but Don thought Joey to be pretty special. He never told him how he really felt, as he thought there should always be an employer/employee relationship in his workplace. But working with Joey's hours to fit his schedule said a lot.

Joey was really surprised when so many new people came to the drumming. And what was more surprising was that three carloads of drummers came from John's reservation. He expected a few more, but not over twice as many. He could see it was going to be an interesting evening.

Mike was quite surprised too. He welcomed everyone and again called upon Joey to offer some words to Great Spirit. Joey agreed, and letting everyone become silent, he said, "We thank you, Great Spirit, for being with each of us. We know we are all One in your great Oneness, therefore let us drum tonight as One, and we know You will help us as we drum."

Mike said "Amen." and turned the session over to John.

John, who was inwardly moved and not saying a word, began drumming; then he started singing. Others he brought with him began drumming too and joined him in chorus. They drummed as One, their voices beautifully pitched to every vocal inflection. It was moving and posed as a model for Mike's group to attain. In an offbeat, John waved his drumstick for everyone to join in. Gradually everyone was in synch, drumming as One. Words in that moment were of little value. Joey loved the resonant feeling within. He looked around and saw many drumming with their eyes closed. The singing and drumming ended. Presently John said, "I hope you will forgive me for not saying anything before beginning, but I felt Great Spirit's Presence deeply and just had to start drumming."

So the session started on a high spiritual tone. John reviewed a couple of songs he had taught them for the benefit of the newcomers. They drummed and sang, and the newcomers were feeling more like they were a part of the group. When they finished, John nodded to Mike and Mike turned to Joey and said, "I think there are so many here because all of us want to learn how drumming can bring feelings of Oneness, Joey. We're all feeling like we're connected right now, so maybe I should be quiet and let you begin."

Joey wasn't quite sure how to begin, so in his openness he was surprised when he said, "About two weeks ago, the Elders advised me to study the words that the Great White Shaman spoke 2000 years ago. I had never read the Bible before. How many here have read Jesus' words?" Half in the hall raised their hands. "What do you think Jesus' most important teaching is?"

There was kind of a long hesitancy. Finally someone said, "To love one another."

Joey said, "Right on. Why do you suppose 'Love ye one another' is the most important of all His teachings?" Again there was a long pause before someone said, "Well, you said when you experienced Light, you also experienced a great love that was a thousand times greater than you had ever experienced, and you said that in that love everything you looked at and thought of was also love. I've wondered about that ever since you said it. Do you think that's why you consider love to be Jesus' most important teaching?"

That sparked a big smile out of Joey, and he said, "Exactly. There is nothing more important than love. Love is really all there is. To tell you the truth, since that experience I've come to realize great love is really what every single person wants in life, but they don't know that it is love that they desire. People try to satisfy their longings by getting the many things the world offers. Our people drum because they feel something is missing in their lives. I know this because during the last meeting I was able to let go of my thoughts which allowed me to experience my Oneness with everyone who was present. And in Oneness, it was that great love that bound us all together as One. It's just about the best experience we can have." Laughing he said, "That's why I wanted to drum again. Drumming helps us to let go of our thoughts." He paused to let that sink in.

It was John who spoke, saying, "I've talked with my friends here about our thoughts, and we've all wondered about our thoughts. Do our thoughts get in the way of experiencing the love you speak of?"

Joey thought for a bit before answering. He wanted to be as precise as he could be, but he also didn't want anyone to feel hopeless about not being able to let go of their thoughts. So he started by saying, "Our thoughts govern our lives. If we have only good thoughts toward everyone and everything, we will enjoy feeling good and will have happiness in this world in spite of what is going on around us.

"My wife, Winnie, is a very good example of this. To tell the truth, I've never heard her say anything negative about anyone, nor have I ever heard her say anything sad or bad about world conditions. Her mother couldn't help but name her Jennifer WindSong in her first days on Earth. That's what she is, a refreshing breeze in life. I try to copy her ways because they're so good. Her way is a beautiful way to be. She has told me that she often gets still to experience the great love that is within her. She does this by letting go of her thoughts in order that the higher part of herself which is Great-Spirit-love, can be her experience. She is a very rich lady in many ways. I hope she doesn't mind that I've shared her private life with you. She's such a good example of being able to let go of her thoughts; I just had to share."

John again spoke saying, "From what you've just said, it's necessary to let go of all thoughts in order to experience the greater love that is within us; is that true?"

Joey replied, "Yes. It seems that when our minds are busy thinking thoughts, our thoughts actually block the heart from opening. What I've learned is that we don't control the greater love that flows from our heart. This greater love has a much greater intelligence than our own conscious intelligence. We try to live life from the thoughts we think, and consciously we don't know about life. We learn a little bit about life from our experiences, and that's about it. So when we with our minds think thoughts without the heart's intelligence which fully knows life, we are like a ship sailing on a sea without a rudder. So with our minds, we can learn to have only good thoughts which makes life a lot happier, because our thoughts are more in line with our heart's intelligence. Using one of the Great White Shaman's teachings again, Jesus also said, '*Seek to know the truth, and the truth shall set you free.*' What He meant was, seek to know the truth of your Being which is Great Spirit Itself, and the experience of the Truth that you are will set your mind free from the need to think thoughts, simply because the mind is not capable of putting the Reality of the Great Spirit into thoughts or words. Great Spirit cannot be reduced to words." Then Joey thought to add, "Jesus also said, '*You must be perfect, even as your Father in heaven is perfect.*' Now, there is no way that any of us can be perfect on our own, so we must be open to let Great Spirit express its perfection through us, which is another good reason why we must let go of our thoughts. Can you see why we need to let go of our thoughts?"

John gave Joey an approving look and said, "I'm beginning to see what you mean."

Joey looked at Mike and asked if it was time for a break, and Mike said, "Okay."

Joey thought if all of this about the thoughts that we think was new to everyone, then time was needed for a little digestion to take place. Although Joey was young in age, he was not young in knowing how to handle his own thought life. He had learned at an early age how not to let those long-seeing detrimental incidents that people were going to experience, affect him. And he had that sudden realization that he created his own fear thoughts, and that he could control his own world of thought. It was a tremendous realization that allowed him to be in control of his life. He knew that people were entirely oblivious to their own thoughts and how thinking affected their worlds, which is why he thought it was time for a break. The thinking about thoughts he knew to be a huge subject for everyone.

After an interim of time which gave people a chance to reconnect with the world they were familiar with, a lone drumbeat sounded to bring everyone together again. Others picked up their drums and joined in the rhythmic cadence of the sound. When the leader stopped, all the others stopped too.

Joey took the opportunity to point out how all the individual drums sounded as one drum. "Think," he said, "if all the drums were actually the thought of each one in the world loving everyone else, what would the feeling be like in the world?" He let that idea sink in. "Do you think there would be any room for discord?" Again, he let the idea register. "This is why love is the most important feeling you can experience. When you elevate your mind to the level of love, you simply start vibrating on a higher level which allows your Light to become brighter. I don't know if this is true or not, but you might say that Light is love being visible. For sure love and Light are One. Both are of Great Spirit and Great Spirit is One. There are no two Great Spirits. Each of us has the choice to think whatever kind of thoughts we want to think. Why not think the best thoughts we can, in order to be as close to Great Spirit as we can? Can you think of anything greater than being One with Great Spirit?" He could see them all ponder on what he said. "I don't know if I've answered all your questions. Anyone?" Nobody said anything. "It's really good to remember that we have a responsibility for the thoughts we think, that responsibility is to our own self. Thoughts are our own conscious creations, and the question that is always before us is, how beautiful do we want our lives to be? The world out there and our own circumstances in it cannot alter our choice to have a beautiful world within ourselves if we so choose. With our thoughts we are creators in our own right." He thought he should stop there. If anyone had a question, he or she could speak up, but none did. Then

Joey thought to say, "I know that our thoughts are the major part of our lives, if anyone feels the need to discuss anything that you don't understand, call me and I'll try to help you. One thing we all want is clarity of mind, because with clarity we rest in understanding." With that he felt he closed his part of the meeting. He looked at Mike.

Mike took the cue and said, "I think we've all had an eventful evening. Thank you, Joey. You've given us a lot to ponder. Now if anyone needs a drum, please see me, and I'll help you. Thanks for coming and I hope you'll all come again." With that they started to disburse.

Joey had put the question how they thought and what they thought right in their laps. Each knew there was no way they could dodge what he had said. And each would in time enlarge his or her understanding by recognizing and changing their thought life where needed. Some would find love growing on the heels of new understanding, for understanding spiritual things enlightens the mind, which makes for loving the new way of thinking, because it makes life feel ever so much better. Many thanked Joey individually, and one in particular had Joey's attention so fully that John and his group, not wanting to interrupt, left without having a personal chance to thank him. Joey had given them a lot to consider, and it would take some time for each one to get used to the practice of observing their own thoughts, which would allow their lives to take on a lot more meaning. Each would find in time that they were waking up to seeing that the quality of their thinking was what life was all about.

On the way home, Joey felt he had shared all the main topics of spiritual information that were helpful. Perhaps some would feel the urge to read or re-read Jesus' words, which would cause them to go within to understand His true meanings. Emphasis was on how thoughts affected their lives. And he gave thanks for having been led to say what he thought were the right words. He was becoming more and more aware of an accentuated strength when sharing before a group, and that was giving him a growing confidence in the words he was sharing. He didn't know how this was occurring. He was just aware that he was having help and was grateful for it.

He pulled into his drive to find Winnie still up and waiting for him. It was always a pleasure to see her happy smile greet him. He told her he had used her ways of meditating in order to get across the point of being able to let go of the mind to experience the love that poured forth from the heart, saying that he hoped that she didn't mind him doing that. He said it just seemed to pour out of him. She was surprised, but said it was okay. She had not been present so it really could not affect her, for her mind did not personally concentrate on herself very much. She could easily see that anyone could be used as an example if they meditated like she did. So she said to Joey smiling, "Just be careful how much you share about our personal life. We don't want imaginations to soar."

Joey looked back at her smiling the words, "Don't worry."

Then she said, "Oh, I almost forgot to tell you. Sally called tonight. It seems she wants to put together a much larger gathering for you to speak to if you're interested. I told her I'd have you call her. We talked some about True, and that was it."

Right off Joey knew what his answer would be, and told Winnie, "Here we go again. It looks like we're going to be busier and busier." He was pretty sure that he had opened a door for a lot of inquiries about the huge truth of everyone being love and Light, which, in turn, also triggered the need to know how to make their love and Light identity become a knowing in their life.

When he called Sally the next evening, he learned that the people who were there at Sally's home were very impressed with what he had shared with them. Subsequently they had really spread the word around about what they heard. "The feeling in which you shared it caused an interest that has been growing all the time," Sally said. "Mainly, there are many now who want to hear you speak. That's the feedback I'm getting. I feel the time is right to hold a big meeting for that to happen. If you feel the same way, then we can go ahead and make plans."

Joey asked, "How many do you think would attend?"

"I think at least three times as many as were at my place." Sally replied.

Joey then asked, "Do you have a date and time in mind?"

Sally said, "In about 3 or 4 weeks."

Joey said, "Okay. I'll look at my schedule and get back to you, possibly tomorrow or the next day for sure."

Sally said, "Okay, and thanks. I'll look for your call." Joey and Winnie looked at what they had scheduled and decided on a date between Thanksgiving and about one week into December would work. Anything before or after that period would be too much into the holidays. So Joey called Sally back to let her know so she could make the necessary arrangements.

Joey had hardly left the reservation to speak when he had a long-seeing experience for himself--the first one he ever had that pertained to him rather than to somebody else. He was given the knowing that he would be speaking to many White groups in the times ahead. And in that long-seeing, he saw many waking up to their Great Spirit nature, and this heartened him deeply. By the time he arrived, he was in a very joyful mood.

CHAPTER 15

INTO THE WHITE WORLD AGAIN

THE BIG SIGN ON THE front read Women's Auxiliary League. He entered and introduced himself to two ladies sitting at a table; one called to Sally, and she immediately came over and greeted Joey with a big hug, telling him how good it was to see him again. She took him around to introduce him to some of her friends. Roger saw Joey and came over to say hello shaking his hand, saying that he was beginning to understand his being Light and love, and was glad he was going to share that information again. "You are, aren't you?" he asked. Joey nodded yes. They talked some to catch up, giving Joey a chance to let go of some of the apprehension he was feeling.

Time goes by swiftly before a session begins, and he thought as he was being introduced there were about 75-80 in the audience.

Many of the tribes he had spoken to were of that size, so the number was not new. He guessed that part of the advertising of his being Indian was responsible for part of the draw. Down deep he was grateful that he had been given a long-seeing vision that he would be helpful to his brothers and sisters of all races. Truth is the truth that applies to all. Sally in the introduction said, And now I'd like you to meet Joey, or Joseph Long-Seeing as his parents named him. Joey?"

Adjusting the mic Joey started, "You know, I think that's the first time I've ever been introduced as Joseph Long-Seeing-- sounds kind of Indian, doesn't it? There was some acknowledgement, and he felt the audience to be engaged with his words. "I'm really happy to be here this evening. I consider it a privilege that I have the opportunity to share with you what is vital to everyone. Most of you know or have heard that I've had a beautiful Light and love experience that has revealed to me my true spiritual identity or true nature. Would you like me to tell you about it?" The response was unanimous. And so he recounted to them all that happened that evening about 13-14 months ago.

He then shared with them what the Elders had told him about everyone on Earth being in a new cycle of time of higher energies where everyone was leaving behind the old way of people living off of each other to a new way of creative sharing. This new cycle of time would be one of living from the heart instead of trying to live from the mind, which was responsible for the heart-aches of man down through all the past civilizations. All previous civilizations have failed, simply because they didn't know their true Light and love connection to Great Spirit and to each other. Then he said, "The heart of each of you is already One. You are not separate from each other, and the truth being known, you do not have an individuality as such. As Great Spirit is One, all of humanity is really One. There is no separation in Spirit, and you are Great Spirit that wants to express Its light and love through you"

If you read your Bible, in Genesis 1, it says that man was created in the image and likeness of God or Great Spirit which is the same thing. As Light and love, you are greater than you've ever known yourself to be. The truth of who you are is very simple, yet the mind wants to make it complicated, simply because the mind wants to be in control with its thinking. Great Spirit is way too high to be reduced to words. It simply cannot be done. The main use of mind is meant to process events or activities in our lives, whereas mind used synchronistically with Great Spirit is unfathomable in achieving Its high spiritual purpose.

"For a long, long time, much longer than any of us knows, man has tried to live by what he sees with his mind, and everyone has perceived differently. Each of us sees this world in our own way. When we look at the world, we think what we're seeing is real. Our senses report to us what we visibly see, and we trust our senses. This gives us the strong tendency to see the outer world to be more real than the Great Spirit that we cannot see. So in a way, our senses trick us, whereas in the Indian culture our people knew, and still know to some degree, that Great Spirit lives in everything--all the animals, the trees and vegetation, the waters, all the Earth, sky, sun, moon and all the heavenly bodies. All is of the Great Spirit and is the Great Spirit. There isn't anything that Great Spirit is not. They had to know this, because they had to respect everything around them, for if they did not and wasted the resources that supported them, they would die.

"So in this new cycle of time we're now in, we're going to see and know Earth life as it truly is. Gone will be theories of all kinds, both scientific and religious, all suppositions, all guessing. We will come to know as God knows, because we will shift from the mind being the leader to letting our hearts be the leader. All hearts contain the same One truth--that Great Spirit is the love and Light of our Being. As I said earlier in describing the great love that I experienced, love sees and knows whatever love looks upon to also be love. As there is no separation in Light and no separation in love, we will no longer feel separate from each other. We will know ourselves to be One.

"This new cycle of time that we're in is the good news. Love and Light will prevail. Everyone is still the love and Light image of Great Spirit. This truth can never change. We all have a likeness to our Creator, and what's beautiful is that we can discover this great truth, because it is in our hearts."

Joey stopped. He knew from previous experience that he had dropped huge, out-of-the-ordinary ideas on his listeners, which had major effects on their thinking. So he signaled to Sally to let her take over. She, in turn, said, "Let's take a short break, and when we come back, we'll get into the interesting question and answer part of the evening." She then passed out pieces of paper on which they were to write their questions.

When everyone settled down, the questions were collected and given to Joey. He just took the one on top and read, "Who are the Elders that you mentioned, and how do you know if they are credible?"

Joey had to backtrack to his Light experience and inject the part the Elders played in the experience to explain what to him was their credibility. He explained how they spoke as an audible voice speaking words in his head, and he offered that they had spoken to him on several occasions since, including about the new time cycle that humanity was now in. Joey felt he had answered the question as fully as he could, so he read the next question.

"I have never seen or felt this light and love that you say all of us are. This is way beyond anything that I've ever thought myself to be. Can you offer some proof other than your own experience?"

Joey was seeing how deeply asleep some in the White world were. He asked who had asked this question. A woman raised her hand. Then looking directly at her he asked, "Have you ever read the

Bible?" And she answered yes. "Well, I think you can recall Jesus' famous words, 'Seek to know the truth, and the truth shall set you free.' Jesus was saying, find the Light and love within yourself, and you will be free of having to live by your thoughts alone. That's about the best testimony I can give to support my experience. I can only be a messenger of the Light and love that I am and share that message as I get a chance." Still looking at the woman, he said, "Does that help?" She nodded yes.

If Joey could know it, his quoting Jesus really stumped her. And many others in the audience were also surprised to hear an Indian quoting Jesus. It made them listen more intently. He was, after all, young and had deeply colored skin, which did not lend to someone speaking with authority. But the naturalness and sincerity in his delivery was very hard to disavow.

The next question was, "Will the man I've been living with for several years ever ask me to marry him?" That drew an audible murmur from the audience.

Joey said, "Good question, but I'm sorry that I do not have the power to be able to help you. Whatever I see for others is given to me. I have no control in seeing the long-seeing events of what I'm going to see."

The next question was stunning, for he had not mentioned anything about True Son. Joey read, "I've heard that you have a White son who came to you mysteriously to replace your own son who was stillborn on that same day. Can you tell us about that?"

"Well, yes I can. He's quite a bit to handle--he's into everything!" Joey exclaimed. "He was a big surprise package in our life...." He told them the whole emotional story and that took some time. By the time he finished, the audience was identifying very closely with Joey, which put a deeper level of acceptance on his message. The tenderness of a small child kind of enveloped the audience into a feeling of cohesiveness.

Joey saw Sally getting his attention, so he said, "We just have time for one more question." He read from the small piece of paper, "Everyone thinks thoughts all the time, which makes all our lives different. How will the thoughts of everyone ever get together so that everyone will be together in like thinking in this new cycle of time you say we're in?"

Joey thought that to be a huge question, and he found himself saying before he thought of saying the words, "Just as you have asked the question, others will also ask the same question, until eventually everyone will come to learn that they are the love and Light of Great Spirit, the Creator of us all. I don't see any great significant answer that will satisfy everyone. Most everyone here has a lot to think about. That's what new information does, it makes us think. In my own experience, for which I had no previous forewarning of any kind, I did a lot of thinking afterward, as you will think upon what I've shared with you this evening. If you don't, you are bound to bump into this information again, for in time it will be main-stream in our world. The truth of everything will win out. This is the last question I'll answer. Is anyone not clear on what I've just said?"

One person said aloud, "This is so huge. It seems far beyond being a possibility."

Joey said, "The message that you are love and Light is much greater than anything the mind can imagine. I suggest that you think about how great you are, and let the rest go, for as you know, you can go all over the place with your mind arguing for this and arguing for that, which will lead you nowhere. Keeping yourself centered on your true identity is the only way you'll find out who and what you are. If you need help, look to what Jesus has said. All His teachings are about directing us inward to the love and Light that we are. He gave us the example that He was not a personal self, the same as we are not actually a personal self, when He said, 'Foxes have holes, and birds have nests, but the Son of Man has nowhere to *lay his head,'* meaning that He was always integrally One with His Heavenly Father. He always knew and always rested His mind in His true identity.

"He indicated that we are Christ like as He knew Himself to be Christ, since at another point He said, *'You, therefore, must be perfect, even as your heavenly father is perfect.'* He always gave credit to His Heavenly Father for everything. In truth, we are no less than Him. Great Spirit wants to express its perfection through each one of us as love and Light. So it's really not about using our mind to pose obstructions for ourselves. It's for us to examine and study His words, for they direct us inward to learn how vast and how wonderful we are as love and Light." He waited a moment and seeing no one else offering a comment, he turned the meeting back to Sally.

Sally took the opportunity to thank Joey, and all strongly applauded him. Joey was becoming good at speaking to an audience. It was one thing to get a message across, but it was another thing to have the message register and stay with those who heard it. Joey always spoke from his heart which carried a feeling impact. Taking on a life of its own, his message of being light and love spread fan-like outside the reservations. The fact that it was coming from a young Indian made it all the more intriguing. It was resonating in young hearts and minds with its awakening energy.

With no visible hope for corrections in any of the current world situations, receptivity for solutions to the problems was increasing everywhere, which was like fertile soil for new ideas. For it is known to the understanding mind that when civilizations reach a point where their operating systems no longer provide for further expansions, new and greater information is required for the civilization's continuance. That is the great lesson that all the previous civilizations failed to employ. Joey was not a historian, but he knew that love and Light is what the world needed.

Sally, in saying goodbye to Joey, and giving him an envelope that was quite thick said, "I have a feeling after what you told us this evening, many are going to want to learn more from you. I know I grasped the truth of your light and love experience right away when you shared it with Roger and me at your home, but I've had to do some deep pondering and thinking of how to make that become a reality in my life. I know it's only been a few months since then, but I feel like I need more instruction. I feel certain others will also want further instruction too."

Joey, having given Sally a big thank you for the gift she gave him, thought for a moment and said, "I know what you mean. The most help I can give at the moment is to get still, let the mind slow down, for Spirit has to have room in your mind to reveal itself to you in just the right way that is right for you. Keeping Great Spirit in mind during your free-from-responsibility-moments helps a lot in changing your consciousness from what you've been thinking to have more of a conscious spiritual consciousness. All of us have to let go of our thinking so that Spirit can speak to us in its own way. That we do by learning to get still. This takes practice and diligence. Does that help for now?"

She said, "I've tried to do that, but my mind is so busy, I don't seem to get it to slow down. Thoughts keep coming."

Joey said, "I know. We're so used to relying on our thinking for everything that our thought-life, if I can use that term, is the problem for each of us. Our thoughts seem like they're a huge problem, because in a certain way we try to fight against them, and this is not really what we want to do. Our thoughts stream forth from our subconscious and they have life, which is why we can't go against their energy easily. I suggest you just try watching your thoughts without reacting to them. Just watch them, and they'll gradually slow down. In getting still, we are looking to be relaxed, and we get really relaxed when the mind gets relaxed. Be aware of where there might be tensions in your body. Tensions are caused by our thoughts.

"Also, while you're watching your thoughts, see if there are repetitions of those thoughts that give you concern by the feelings you have about them. See if those repetitive thoughts are something like issues you might be dealing with, such as all people, past and present, situations, conditions which concern you in everyday life. Notice your feelings. If you don't like the feelings, this is a good sign that you might need to change your thinking to have better thoughts than the ones that are giving you those not-so-good feelings.

"Most everyone has difficulty initially when trying to get still. But keep trying and you will have success. Make it a steady effort to get your mind still. It doesn't take much time when we're first starting, and as you find that you like getting still, you will easily increase the time of your practice because you'll find it so beneficial. Does that help at all?"

Sally said, "Yes. I can see how that will be helpful--kind of the opposite from what I've been doing."

Joey offered also, "It's what I've had to do, and it helped me." He then said, "Well, I've got a little drive, so I'd best be going. Thanks for setting up this evening. It's been fun. Call me if I can be of further help."

Sally said, "Thank you for coming. I think we'll be in touch."

Joey reflected on the way home that it had been a successful evening and thanked Great Spirit for the opportunity to share with others. It had been interesting to be in an all White gathering, not really any different than being with his own race, for he knew all were of the One Spirit.

Winnie was still up wanting to know how it went. Joey told her all about it while counting out the $350 Sally had given him. That was a nice surprise. That would add to True's savings account which had over $2600 in it. Winnie said, "Part of my staying up is to tell you of the funny call I got this evening. It was a man's voice, who said 'If you know what's good for you, you'll stay on your own reservation.' That's all he said and hung up."

"About what time did he call?" asked Joey.

"I think it was about 9:00. Why do you ask?"

"I have a feeling the call was from someone here on the res."

"What makes you think that?"

"I'm not sure. It was just a strong thought that flashed across my mind. I'll have to think about it, and if need be, I'll get quiet maybe to get some insight or get an answer." Joey also said, "I don't think it's anything to worry about."

Winnie said, "I sure hope you're right."

Joey then offered, "I think if I were going off the res on a regularly scheduled basis, we'd have to be concerned. Maybe it's someone who thinks that we're not supposed to share our message with the White world. If so, then maybe he can be spotted." Winnie was pleased that Joey was putting deductive logic behind his reasoning. Still, she was apprehensive since she had received the call.

CHAPTER 16

THE GIFT OF A LIFETIME

FIRST CHANCE JOEY GOT, HE asked Charlie if he knew anyone on the res who was opposed to his speaking to White groups. He didn't tell Charlie about the phone call Winnie had received. No use circulating that around the res. Charlie didn't know of anyone, but he would ask around.

Christmas was coming, so Joey and Winnie considered whether it was wise or not to open True up to Christmas ideas of receiving toys and the like. They decided they didn't want to get into that this year; he was too young for that anyway. They were pretty sure they didn't want True to be affected by something so fictional and materialistic. They were keeping the TV away from True. They might change their minds later, but that was their view for the present. They knew that in the near future when True would start to ask about Christmas, they would have to somehow keep resentment and judgment out of the picture if they didn't change their minds later. Giving or "potlatching" was a year-round event for Indians anyway, so they weren't without an attitude of giving. So they shared their feelings with their mothers to make sure they understood. Grandmothers can be very soft-hearted.

There were so many things to consider in raising True; how to keep him normal in every respect and yet shield him from being involved with unnecessary world affairs. They didn't want worldly influences adversely affecting his spiritual remembering. The Elders had said that True would remember himself as a spiritual being and to support him. This they considered their first responsibility. They often wondered openly between themselves, when would True start to show signs of remembering his knowingness as Spirit? They already knew he had inner sight that allowed him to see into other dimensions. They felt their responsibility for True was a higher cut above parents who were raising a normal child--so much more to be alert to and to care about. True was running around in high gear, and they felt he would soon be starting to talk.

In about 16 months Joey's spiritual understanding had expanded phenomenally. Some dedicated seekers never gain as much spiritual knowing in their whole lives. Plus he had gained great wisdom by speaking to so many tribes. Now he was starting to go out into the White world to speak; another high learning curve was beginning. It was remarkable to watch someone expand in spiritual consciousness so rapidly without becoming personally affected in some strange way. Joey just became more and more natural as he radiated happiness. His happiness was infectious when he shared the message that everyone was the love and Light of their Creator. That made audiences believe that love and Light was real. Joey didn't realize that he was lucky that he didn't have deeply ingrained issues to work through in his life like most have while seeking the Truth within themselves.

His pure love for Winnie was a big reason his heart opened so easily in his Light experience. And Winnie expanded in consciousness right along with him. As two souls, both were well suited for their spiritual work. And it was just beginning.

Charlie's Fund had grown to over $20,000. All on the committee were deeply amazed that in a few months the Fund had grown so much, and it showed that recent deposits had been made. The Fund was getting in reach of being used, and that was making it very exciting. Opinions were pretty strong regarding how to tell Joey and Winnie what they were about to receive. Opinions led to discussion and discussion turned to the idea of how each one of them would feel if they were receiving a new home. That put the right twist on it, all of them saying that they personally would like to have some input on what was to be their new home. All were in agreement and felt that Joey and Winnie should be making the decision. That way there wouldn't be any chance for ill feelings to develop.

Then, where could the home be set up? There were several locations where mobile homes had previously been located. This would be a matter for the Tribal Council to decide. This would be the first time anyone outside of the committee would know about giving Joey and Winnie a new home. And again, everyone concluded that Joey and Winnie should be in on the decision where their new home should be located.

First they would have to make sure the Fund would cover all costs. They would have to make a list of the available Mobile Homes--the prices of each etc. Then they would have to consult with the Tribal Council. When all the details were worked out, the costs, the locations, etc., then they could tell Joey and Winnie. Someone suggested that maybe the appropriate way to tell them would be to have a dinner in their honor. It would signify the grand occasion, for all the Tribes were a part of it. Everyone agreed that the presentation of a new home was a grand occasion and that a dinner in their honor was a good way to do it. Someone said, "Charlie and the teen-agers should be invited too. They're a big part of this. And what about the Tribal Council? Shouldn't they officially be here?" All pondered the ideas and agreed that to make it right, all of them should be invited. It would be part of honoring Joey and Winnie properly. It was getting more and more exciting.

Christmas came and went. Three on the committee had made the rounds of mobile home sales locations and had come up with a list of possible homes to choose from, some of them pretty nice three bedroom, 28-feet-wide units. The Fund had grown substantially before Christmas. Money-wise they were now in the ball park. The Tribal Council had been consulted, and a list of possible site locations was organized, one of which was exactly where Joey had sat on a stump to gather himself after his Light experience, but this was not known to anyone. A date was set in the evening in the middle of January and everyone concerned was invited to attend.

When Charlie was told about the dinner, he was kind of the lead ex-officio member of the committee, on how they were going to present the gift of a new home to Joey and Winnie. He was asked if he would be the one to invite them. This choked Charlie up a little, and he thought that maybe he was the right one to do it. So far as he knew neither Joey nor Winnie knew anything about the Fund. Charlie thought a moment before saying okay, and then he said, "I think I will say to Joey that the tribe wants to honor him and Winnie with a dinner, so that they will know that it is a special occasion for them, but they will know nothing about receiving a new home. What do ya' think?"

The member thought a bit and said, "I think it'll work." So it was a happy Charlie who invited Joey and Winnie to their honorary dinner.

The honorary dinner for Joey and Winnie was less than a week away. They didn't know what to make of this special dinner that was in their honor. Joey knew that his Light experience which triggered potlucks and drumming sessions, was deeply appreciated by all on the reservation, but he didn't feel that a special dinner was needed, because he could feel the gracious energy that came from the people as he moved among them. This wondering for a couple of days troubled him, but then he thought, if they want to show their gratitude by having a dinner for us, we'll just accept it. He talked with Winnie about his feelings, and she said in response, "The dinner is all set. They're expecting us, so we'll just go and enjoy the moment. I guess these things are just what people like to do." Joey nodded his head in agreement. Little did they know the great surprise that was waiting them.

The days before the dinner went by quickly. Joey put the bag that Winnie loaded up to take care of True's needs in the truck bed, and they were at the Community Hall before they knew it. When they walked in, they saw dinnerware had been set up on table cloths; it all looked pretty fancy. The dinner began with one of the committee members thanking Joey and Winnie for coming, saying, "I hope you like roast elk. I got my elk this fall and this is the best way I know to share it. Let's everyone in their own way give thanks to Great Spirit that Joey, Winnie and True Son live on this reservation." There was silence for a few moments. Then there was a thank you from everyone, and all said with practically one voice, "Amen." It was a scrumptious meal. Joey thought getting honored with such a fine meal was pretty good. He had never tasted elk with all the trimmings before. It was all very delicious to his palate. Winnie thought it excellent also, especially since she didn't have to cook--something men don't have to think about very much, if hardly at all.

When everyone had finished their brownie and ice cream dessert, Charlie, who had been chosen to present the gift, got up to say, "You know I'm not much of a speaker, but Joey and Winnie, you know how much all of us love both of you. You have given my life back to me, and all on the res are deeply grateful for the good medicine (those words slipped out again) you have brought to our whole tribe. Have you heard of Charlie's Fund?"

Joey replied, "A little bit; that's all."

"Well," Charlie continued, "it was actually started by the five teen-agers sitting at the end of your table. Would you young fellas please stand up?" Everyone gave them a big hand.

One of them blurted out, "That's right, Charlie, but you asked us to."

Charlie replied motioning them to sit down, "So I did, but you fellas pushed it, otherwise it never would have started by itself. Joey and Winnie, all of us know how cramped you've been in your 10-foot-wide mobile, so the Fund the boys started was to buy you a new home, which got named Charlie's Fund. Enough money has been sent to the Fund from all the tribes up and down this side of the mountains to buy you a new home. They've all given to your Fund in appreciation for all you've done for them without any solicitation." Joey and Winnie could not believe their ears! This was an unbelievable story that Charlie had just told them! Could this really be true? Joey leaned over to kiss Winnie. He didn't know what else to do.

Charlie continued, "Members of the committee have visited a number of mobile homes sales lots and have come up with a list of homes that you can select from. You can make arrangements with them to select one. And now it's the Tribal Council's turn to speak."

A Council member got up and said, "Joey and Winnie, we're almost as dumbfounded as you are. Our Council had no idea that a

Fund of this nature was developing. We're so happy for you, and we thank you for what you've done for our tribe. There are a number of empty sites where mobile homes were once located. You can have your choice of where you want your new home to be set up." He then went to Joey's table and gave him a map of the reservation where those sites were located. Astonishment after astonishment was stunning their minds! Their eyes were heavily moistened with tears. This was unbelievable; to be given a new home was beyond one's imagination. Then through his tears Joey recognized one of the sites to be right at the place of his light experience. Now tears were running down his cheeks. This was overwhelming! How had all this happened without him having had a clue to what was going on? He thought that people were sure good at keeping secrets.

Everybody was looking at Joey and Winnie. All Joey could say in a choked voice was, "Thank you everyone. This, I could never have expected in a million years. This is overwhelming to say the least!" Winnie struggled to say thank you too. Then Joey said, "This is the greatest gift we could ever receive. Thank you again. The three of us are going to feel liberated. We'll be able to stretch our arms out and not hit walls. Thank you ever so much. This is all really hard to believe!"

At that, the meeting started to break up. Everyone came over to shake their hands. Charlie introduced the five teen-agers to Winnie and Joey. They hadn't known that these five good-looking teen-agers had found sobriety through Charlie's sobriety. The teens thanked Joey for his Light experience that rubbed off on Charlie, which in turn rubbed off on them. They took special notice of True Son too. It was moving to both Winnie and Joey to learn that True Son had had such a profound effect upon them.

This would be an evening they would remember for the rest of their lives. It had been special in every aspect. The ladies who served the meal even gave them some of the left-over elk to take home.

There was no question that Winnie and Joey could not help but feel like they were celebrities. They had a hard time accepting the idea that so many in other tribes had given out of their hearts in such a magnificent way. Joey had no idea that his talks had such a huge effect on so many. It was kind of mystifying to him. He was learning that Light and love had an unparalleled effect on helping people. He knew it wasn't him. He knew that he was just the messenger of Light and love. Silently he gave thanks to Great Spirit for this great bonanza. Before he and Winnie left, one of the committee members made arrangements with them for when they could visit the sales offices to make their selection of a new home. It was agreed that Joey and Winnie would follow in their truck. True Son would ride better that way they thought.

At the appointed time, they left as a caravan of two to go to the first sales office. They looked over what had been selected and said that maybe they would like to go to the next location which was about 30 miles away. They looked at what had been selected at that next location and again said maybe they would like to visit the next location that was another 35 miles away. When they arrived, right away, both of them saw one that took their eye from the outside. They asked if this was on their selected list, and it was. When they went inside, they felt almost instantly that this is what they wanted. It was 28 feet wide, had three bedrooms, two baths, a real nice kitchen, a large eating area and large living room all in an openness, and it looked very new. This was going to suit them well. The three of them all hugged together., which made True feel like he was being crushed. What a delightful surprise! They talked with the two members about what they had to do and were told that they would probably have to sign some papers later, and the sales agent said that would work, as he could see that True was getting restless and that they were eager to leave. The two said they would take care of everything and would talk to them later. It was a very happy

Winnie and Joey who needed to get home to feed True. Both of them were smiling all the way home. Joey had told Winnie where he would like it set up. She was in total agreement with him, and it was right on the edge of the res and close to where Joey could walk to work and come home for lunch. How perfect could it get?

When their new home would get set up on the site they had selected, Joey found that it wouldn't take too much to clean up the yard when spring came. There had been a lawn in the front and back. In the meantime he could pick up the trash as time allowed. In a couple of weeks, they moved in. They didn't have much to move, but that was about to change. Money was still being received into the Fund, and they learned they could use it to buy the furniture they needed and some of the outdoor things, like a lawn mower and storage shed--more wonderful blessings. They weren't even 21 and they had a truck and a home free and clear. It was unbelievable to them. Their gratitude to Great Spirit was a mile high. Most of all, they were grateful for the expanded space in which to live; they felt like they had been liberated, but they would always reflect on how fortunate they were to have had a small place in which to live rent free. They had so many blessings both thought to be unbelievable. They lived their lives in gratitude for all they had.

True was about 18 months old, and he would be getting his own bed soon. They hadn't yet talked about how his room should be decorated, but this idea appeared to them in a very short time. Joey and Winnie felt that he should have something or some things that would help him in remembering his spiritual knowing. Very unexpectedly the Elders said, **"Regarding the way you should decorate your son's room, don't be too concerned. Put a little of everything in it, and he will choose what interests him."** That's all they said. To Winnie and Joey, that made good sense and made it easy to do. It seemed to them the situation would take care of itself. They laughed a little, both agreeing that maybe they were being too concerned beforehand. That Elderly advice gave them an understanding that they didn't have to be so all-the-time conscious about True. They found it relaxing to just let whatever was to unfold, unfold on its own.

Getting used to their new abode was interesting to watch. Initially they had a lot more space than they knew what to do with. Pretty soon, though, both of their mothers were wanting to know how they could help them. The mothers felt that now when they visited, they weren't invading their small space anymore, which made their visits more enjoyable. There were a lot of pluses in their new home. And more room gave both Winnie and Joey some space to be by themselves. The spare bedroom they decided would be the one place where each could be when they needed to be alone. Overall, they were both very happy to be out of those close quarters.

One of the first things they did when they had settled in was to write a letter of gratitude to each tribe that Joey had spoken to. They decided it proper to thank each tribe individually, even though they would do it with a form letter. Joey wrote the letter and picked through his notes on each Tribe to make sure that the letter spoke fully to all the tribes. From his joy-filled heart, it was an easy letter to write. His last line of appreciation was, *"Always feel free to contact me if you think that I can help you in any way."* As one can imagine, that was just the inviting line that many of the tribes, was looking for. And they did. He and Winnie signed it, *"In the light that is always filled with love."*

CHAPTER 17

JOEY GOES HOME

SPRING WAS COMING, AND ALREADY Joey was feeling a connection with Mother Earth as he explored around his yard. The ground under his feet felt vitally different than the yard he had played in growing up. Even though it was still winter, he was more aware of an aliveness in the Earth than he had ever sensed before. He felt sure it wasn't his imagination running away with him, for his mind was at peace. His imagination was not working. What was happening was, he had the feeling of being connected like he was a part of Mother Earth that he was standing on. He couldn't really define it in his mind. It was just something feeling-wise that he couldn't deny. It was such a good feeling, he wanted to share the feeling with everyone, but, of course, he knew it would be very foolish if he tried to do that. But what he did know intuitively was, this is what his ancestors must have felt as they depended on and lived upon the land that provided them with everything. For the first time, he really felt this connection with Mother Earth, is the culture that had been lost during the 400 years of White conquering, as they swarmed across the continent. He felt deep, deep pangs of loss for his people. It couldn't be helped. It was like Great Spirit Life had been ripped away from them.

It was a whole new insight and a whole new understanding that gave Joey a deeper and larger purpose when he would share his message of Light and love with others in future gatherings. He felt that he could now convey his message in a fuller way to the White world too. He also felt he could convey to his own people that they could regain this feeling for Mother Earth in a much deeper way than they possibly were feeling. Everyone didn't just live on Earth, they were an intrinsic part of Earth! Mother Earth energy was a big part of life that was missing in his own life, so he knew that it must also be missing in the lives of almost everyone else.

He felt fortunate that this new experience happened in the winter when everything was still dormant, because if it had happened in the bloom of spring, the feelings of the experience might have mingled with the captivating feelings of warm spring weather and might not have been felt as clearly. He gave thanks to Mother Earth for letting him feel his real connection to her and for providing him and Winnie with all their needs. As usual, first chance he got he shared the experience with Winnie, which she could also partly feel. She volunteered that this experience would be very helpful when True started remembering. Joey smiled like more light was flooding in, saying, "You're right. I hadn't thought of that. This is such a vital part of life. We know that our thoughts are powerful, and our own knowing no doubt will help him remember too." Winnie nodded in agreement.

It seems there was no end to the surprises after they moved into their new expanded quarters. They received a number of cards congratulating them, some with gift cards enclosed. They received flowers and plants. Some even brought sweets and desserts. They felt like they were being showered upon. It all made for extremely good feelings. That went on for a couple of weeks or more. The res was giving abundantly. Even the five teen-agers stopped by with a box of candy. Hearts were resonating in exuberant joy for them, for many knew of the cramped space they lived in and really felt that was not a suitable place where exceptional people like them should have to live. Joey and Winnie could see and feel how much they had influenced others positively on the res. The heartening effect of it registered deeply upon them, and made their love for everyone all the greater.

In a couple of months, True was starting to string his words together. It was a joy for Winnie when he started answering her with sentences and expressed himself with sentences. He had been saying Mommy and Daddy for quite some time and always appeared very bright. Both had watched True seemingly accelerate in all his actions since they moved in. What a blessing their new home was.

It was mid-April. The weather was definitely showing signs of spring after a wintry rainy season that had showed no sign of ever changing, and Joey just got in the door when True ran up to him and wanted to be picked up. With True in his arms, he found Winnie and kissed her and asked, "What's for supper? I think know; I can smell it."

"What else but your favorite, the stew that you love so much." Winnie had learned how to make it from her mother, because Joey had eaten there so much and he always raved about her mother's stew. Then she said, "Oh, you got a call a little while ago from a Samantha Calling Bird who seemed pretty desperate that she talk with you. She mentioned the tribe, but I was busy with True and didn't write it down. Some of them sound so much alike anyways; I wasn't too sure I would get it right, but her number is by the phone."

Joey remarked, "What an interesting name. Maybe I'll learn how she got it." Sometimes while eating, Joey had interesting things to share with Winnie, but nothing happened out of the ordinary that day. They enjoyed the fine stew, after which Joey went outside to do some more clean-up work in the yard. It was turning out to be a bigger job than he had originally thought, plus the grass was beginning to grow, and he wanted to take advantage of the good weather.

After an hour, he went in and finding the number he was supposed to call--listened to the ring, and in short order he heard a woman's voice say, "Hello? Is that you Joey?"

Joey replied that it was and asked, "How can I help you? Winnie said that you sounded urgent?"

The voice said, "Thank you for calling. That's putting it mildly. I'm so glad you called. My name is Samantha Calling Bird. I'm just one in one of the many tribes you've spoken to. Please call me Sammy--everybody does."

"I'm intrigued with your name, Sammy. How did you get to be named Calling Bird?" Joey asked.

"That's part of what I have wanted to talk to you about," she answered. "To fill you in, when I was very small, whenever I went outside, birds would flock around me, sometimes landing on my head and pooping in my hair. I learned to wear a hat. The many different kinds of birds always delighted me. They always made me laugh and giggle. I loved them. But as I grew older they stopped coming; even if I did call them, they wouldn't come. Gradually, I got over my disappointment at their not coming to me."

Joey was amazed at what she had just told him and said, "You mean you didn't actually call the birds to you?" to which she replied that she didn't. Joey was getting more and more interested and thinking that her name was not the main reason for Sammy wanting to talk to him, asked, "What's on your mind?"

"I remembered you telling about the great love you felt coming from your heart while having your Light experience, because just recently I think I experienced that great love also. It's been almost a year since you spoke to us. I wasn't really doing anything or thinking anything that would prompt this love. It just happened, and it was beyond wonderful. I really want to feel that love again. How do I do that?"

Joey thought and it came to him, like flashing thoughts do, that she just might have a spiritual work of some kind to do, so he answered, "I think, but I'm not sure, since you had a gift of birds flocking to you when you were small and you yourself didn't call them to you, I'm thinking that possibly Great Spirit is awakening you through your wonderful inner love experience to be useful in helping your people spiritually in some way."

Sammy responded, "Really? That's awfully hard to believe. I can't even keep the same beat when I'm drumming with others."

"I think I know what you mean," Joey said. Then he offered, "Sammy, it's quite possible that the birds stopped coming to you because as a child your heart was wide open with love, which was why the birds came to you. They enjoyed your love. Then it's possible your mind started thinking about things which shut down the love from flowing out of your heart, and your love not being there, the birds were no longer attracted to you."

Sammy thought a little bit and said, "You could be right. It was right about the time I started school. But what does that have to do with having a spiritual work of some kind?"

Joey replied, "It seems when we're young, we're quite innocent—every one of us is. But as we grow older and learn about the world through the educational system that we have, we lose our innocence.

By starting to think thoughts, our thoughts cover over the happiness of our hearts. We really need to return to our youthful innocence. I suspect that when you drum, you're trying to drum with your mind, whereas you will find that as you let go of your thinking while drumming, you will be right in synch with all the other drummers. Does any of this make sense to you?"

Sammy said thoughtfully, "I follow your reasoning and it makes sense, but letting go of my mind does not sound easy, because that's what I do. I think."

To that Joey said, "Precisely, we all do. That's why we have to acknowledge and accept that our true identity is love and Light. We must bring our thinking around to claim what we really are. By so doing, we begin to change our thinking world to what makes us feel good. Thinking about all that goes on in the world does us no good at all. This is a world of Great Spirit in every way. It's really not a materialistic world at all. You are love and you are Light. Spirit has given you a wonderful love experience to help you remember who and what you really are. Does that help?"

Sammy said, "Yes. That's pretty clear. I think I get it. I don't want to take up any more of your time. But if I get stymied, can I call you again? I really do thank you for helping me."

Joey replied, "Certainly, any time. And really change your thinking. Don't just think about changing your thinking. Okay?"

Sammy thanked Joey again and said, "Okay, and have a nice evening. Bye." There was still some daylight left, and Sammy stepped outside to consider all that Joey had said. As she stood there she noticed a flock of birds fly into the trees. She thought that to be unusual, then another flock flew into the trees. She was really bewildered, when another flock of birds flew into the trees. This was not the season when blackbirds gathered together. What's more, it sounded like every one of them was chirping. Sammy could not dismiss what she was experiencing. She intuitively knew that this was no happen-by-chance experience. Joey had spoken truthfully to her, and now the birds were bidding her to do what Joey had suggested. The wonder of the experience introduced her to the profound ways of Great Spirit, launching her into a whole new era of thinking higher thoughts which, in turn, allowed her to experience the love that she loved so much. Spirit life was coming to the fore on the reservations in many different ways.

Sammy had no way of knowing how deeply her name had affected Joey. When Joey shared with Winnie how she received her name, Winnie saw and felt the wonder in his voice. It was almost like he had experienced birds settling around him. Great was the wonder of Great Spirit's activity of Oneness. Joey was to find, as time went on, he would experience many spiritual rewards for his efforts that would enlarge the scope of his spiritual knowing. Each expansion would be full of joy and appreciation for the wonders that Spirit would bring to him.

A few months went by, and it was True's second birthday. He had a fun day with both grandmothers doting on him. He went around saying, "I'm already two years old. Don't I look it?" He was saying things off the top of his head that made all close by blink. It didn't look like he was going to be difficult in any way in what some little ones suffer in their terrible twos. He seemed to his parents to be always fresh and new, often provoking amusement and laughter. It didn't appear to them that he was going to be a handful in any way in minding what they wanted him to do, but they could see that they were always going to have to pay full attention to him when he was around them. True was a delight to have around; they didn't know what to expect next. It was a good thing the Elders had said that True was going to remember he was Spirit. That had been very good advice. Winnie and Joey were beginning to live in expectation, not exactly like being on edge, but open with awareness to everything that True did. They were finding that was a very interesting way to live. True was their real center of attention, more so than ever.

The days passed by swiftly. It was a perfect early August day; it had been it the low 80's, and Joey felt compelled to step outside to view the starry night sky which he often did. He had always been entranced by the Great Works of the Milky Way as are so many others. On this particular night the atmosphere was exceptionally clear, only a sliver of a new moon was to be seen later. The moon was in the Earth's shadow and was in the closest proximity to the Earth in its elliptical journey around its parent, some 26,000 miles closer than at the time of full moon when the sun's light pressure pushes it away from the Earth. Science will one day discover that the sun's light has pressure, which will then open a whole new area in the discovery of celestial mechanics.

But Joey knew nothing of this as he looked in awe at the heavenly works. The compelling desire to gaze upward in awe always mystified him. This evening was no exception. The cool of the early night added to his entrancement. As he wondered about the possibility of his Creator's intention for the uncountable billions of stars, he suddenly saw and felt them all morph into One. What an exhilarating feeling! The morphing he was experiencing was not a physical happening of all coming together visibly as One, but was what was happening in his consciousness. It was like there was no individuation in all the heavenly bodies he was viewing. They were all aspects of One Great Being. He felt insignificant like a little child being a part of a greatness of the Oneness that he was experiencing, while at the same time he felt the greatness of Being the Whole! The feeling was so ultra-grand that he couldn't wrap his mind around it. Mentally there was nothing compared to it. The whole of the experience elevated his mind to experience the knowing that everything was contained as One in the Great Mind of Spirit. He felt touched by that which has no definition, which he would later come to understand that it was what the Indians referred to as the Great Mystery, out of which everything had come into existence. To say the least, it was overwhelming to Joey. He just stood there in total amazement, transfixed beyond thought, beyond anything he had ever known. Nothing needed to be explained, nothing could be added to it. To him, he knew everything in creation was being called Home to its original Source. What the mind deems mysterious is but the simple activity of the Creator holding the whole of creation in Itself as One. So simple he thought. Great Spirit was never separate at any time from anyone or anything.

If Joey could have known that he experienced the actuality of The Unified Field Theory or later named the Zero Point Theory which scientific minds had surmised was the active energy within and acting on all matter, he would have been further amazed. This understanding would have given him the insight that science was very close to knowing the Reality of Spirit, which would have been helpful to him in trying to get spiritual points across to his listeners. It would be a few years later that he would gain this understanding and use it to explain how the study of material science has effectively programmed the mind to believe that earthly matter is all that exists, thereby numbing the western mind against learning anything spiritual.

He didn't know how long the experience lasted. It didn't matter. He knew that life's big question had been answered. Everything was Spirit, and Spirit was always redeeming its own. As he thought in wonder of it all, he could not help but see the great futility of all those who knew not of their Spirit Self in trying to make sense of the world by their thinking mind, while at the same time, all was really well within them regardless of what they might be experiencing. So much became clear; so much was spiritually understood. As he felt that he had taken in all that he could understand, he began to notice chilliness in the night air and decided to go inside. When he opened the door, the warm air of the day greeted him, and he gave thanks for his home and for the great experience he just had. He always gave thanks for his home. He never took the great gift for granted. He had become vitally energized by his indescribable experience and wasn't sure if he could sleep, but seeing it was past 11:30, he thought about having to get up early for work in the morning and decided to go to bed. He laid himself gently down in bed, trying not to disturb Winnie, but found his mind as active as ever in going over his experience. He looked at the alarm clock beside the bed; it was well after midnight. He thought, I can't sleep and started to get up, when Winnie asked to his surprise "Where ya' going?" Joey said, "I didn't know you were awake. I can't sleep, so I was going to the kitchen to get something to eat."

Winnie said, "You know we're not separate. I feel what you feel. I know something great has happened to you. I'd be happy if you'd share it with me."

Once again Joey was amazed at the partner he had. He replied, "Of course, honey." He was happy that he could share what was bursting to come forth from within himself. It was very relieving to try to tell Winnie all of the feelings he had during the experience. This took some time to do, and it turned out that it settled his thoughts down to a point where his eyes started to feel heavy. In a bit, he said, "Goodnight, sweetheart."

Winnie surprised him when she said, "Cuddle me, honey," which he was glad to do.

Her back was to him, so he turned to be close, and as he slid his arm around her waist, she found his hand and pulled it next to her breast so she could feel his hand on her heart. Sleep came easily for both of them.

True climbed out of bed early in the morning and climbed in bed with them before the alarm went off. It was a loving threesome when the alarm broke their interlude of coziness. Joey got up telling

Winnie that she didn't have to get up, but she got up anyway. It was difficult to leave the harmony that he felt so adeptly at home, but during his short walk to work, he felt more alive and closer to everything, plus he was happier than his usual cheerful self. Don didn't pry into Joey's life, but Joey's happiness was infectious, and he finally asked Joey if he had been given another new home, to which Joey replied, "No, but you're close. I feel like I'm Home in God, that's why I'm so happy." Don didn't quite know what to make of Joey's words, so he let it go. But he did know that he felt good because Joey felt so happy, and whatever made Joey so happy was okay with him.

All through the day, everything Joey did felt delightful. Joy was his constant companion all day long. His marvelous experience of Oneness had a long carryover effect. And somehow he knew that everyone in their own time would have the same experience of Oneness of being Home in their Creator. Oneness with the All of everything was a peak experience in the grandeur of feeling, because of love's beautiful unifying quality. Joey was spiritually at Home within himself.

CHAPTER 18

THE WHITE STUDY GROUP

J OEY GREETED THE CUSTOMERS JOYFULLY all day. One man who came in periodically who knew Joey only casually, asked, "What makes you so happy?"

Joey replied unabashedly, "I'm at Home in God."

The customer, surprised said, "You mean Great Spirit?"

Joey said, "Yes. God and Great Spirit are the same. Why do you ask?"

"Well, tell me," the customer asked again, "is God in your heart, or are you in the heart of God?" Joey didn't know the customer was referring to a couple of lines from *The Prophet* by Kahlil Gibran.

Joey thought this conversation was getting interesting. He replied, "Everyone knows there is only One God, therefore there can only be One heart--God's heart, but everyone doesn't know that all live in the heart of God."

The customer, again amazed, recognizing that Joey was right on with his answer, asked further, "How do you know this?"

Joey again very calmly said, "I experienced it"

The customer was really surprised and showed it. Being really impressed, he didn't hesitate in saying, "Sorry to sound like I was interrogating you. My name is George Gaylin, and I'm one in a small group that has been studying spiritual information for several years. We're a little bit familiar with *The Good Red Path* of Indian ways, which is why I asked you if you meant Great Spirit when you answered that you were Home in God. You got my interest up, and that is why I questioned you further. I'm wondering if you would join us some time, and if possible, share your experiences with us? I'm certain the rest of our group would like to hear first hand from you what you've experienced. It would add tremendously to the reality of the truth we've been studying."

Joey hadn't expected this, but his mission came to mind right away and he said, "Yes, I think I could. If you contact me, we can work out the arrangements. My name is Joey."

George got Joey's phone number and said, "Many thanks, I appreciate it, I'll be in touch." and left. George thought 'wow', that's fascinating--someone who has experienced his own inner divinity. He's so young and Indian. George could never have imagined such good luck. He wasted no time in telling those in his group about Joey and piquing their interest, all said they would like Joey to join them.

During his joy fullness that day, Joey began to think that he was only one person and that he couldn't spread himself around to be among all the little truth study groups that might exist; that would be impossible. Sally had already called him a couple of times since he had last spoken at her large public meeting to tell him of the need that others were having for more spiritual guidance, but there weren't any formed study groups that she was aware of, so no meetings were set up for him to attend. But he did learn that others have their respective need for spiritual direction. And he thought too of how Sammy had called him, and how that led her to be aware of a spiritual work that Spirit had in mind for her to do. That made him wonder how many more there were on all the reservations that might be in need of spiritual guidance. If all in both the White and Red world became a personal demand on his time, he knew he could never fulfill all those demands personally, yet he realized that his mission was to try to help everyone wherever he could.

This was a quandary that had lightly crossed his mind from time to time before, but each time he dismissed it as a fancy he was having. But now, here it was staring him right in the face. He was in a dilemma, and he knew his thinking about it couldn't solve it, so he let go of it. No sooner had he let go of it when the idea flashed in his mind like a ball, out of which he saw the need to write a book which he would call *Indian Manifesto - Good Medicine for Good Living*. His first thought was, I'm no writer; this is way out in left field. But he knew that when Spirit gives one something to do, one has no alternative but to do it or at least try. It was then that the Elders spoke saying, **"You can write a book, more like a booklet. Keep it simple."** He was surprised that the Elders had spoken to him at work to confirm his need to write a book.

He was still in joy and wonder when he reached home. Kissing Winnie he said, "You'll never guess what happened to me today." Her look compelled him to tell her. So he told her all the details about George Gaylin and his study group and all the other details that led up to being told to write a book, and what the Elders had said to confirm it.

Winnie said not too surprised, "Well, like you, I too have seen the impossibility of you being able to personally meet everyone's need. It makes sense that you have something to pass along to inquirers, rather than having to say to them, 'I'm sorry, but my schedule is too full.' You know what you want to say, so you will have an easy time writing it."

Joey smiled at Winnie who was always there with the right words, always putting things in the right perspective. Joey said, "It'll be a challenge to learn to write it on the computer." Laughing he continued, "Two challenges, but like all else, step by step and it's not all that hard."

"You got it! Amen." Winnie echoed.

And so began the formulation of words in Joey's mind of what he wanted the booklet to contain. The Elders had said to keep it simple, which Joey knew it had to be. He knew there were only two premises that he wanted to present (1) Only Great Spirit exists, and (2) There is only joy and happiness in life. How to write it in the right words so as to convey the ideas in a complete understanding would be the trick. He felt that would come when he started to write. He could see the back cover with an eagle on it, but the front cover was not there yet. He thought, my little book is almost written, and so he was able to let go of it in his mind.

He discussed it with Winnie saying, "It's going to be such a small booklet, we could never charge for it. Besides it's truth, and we can't charge for truth. How do you feel about our just giving the booklet away? I've thought of sending a copy to all the reservations, which will also keep us in touch with them."

Winnie said right off, "I agree. It's a good idea. We know that life is energy and that we can't put restrictions on how Great Spirit energy is supposed to flow; energy has to flow freely. It's all Spirit energy. Whatever we send out will come back to us. Look at the gifts we've already received, the truck and this house. It'll be a wonderful feeling to just give the booklet away."

George called a couple of days later, wondering if Joey could come to their meeting next Thursday. It was short notice, but seeing his schedule clear, Joey said he could make it. He got directions and time and told Winnie that meeting with six men who have been studying truth for some time was going to be a brand new experience for him. He said he felt like he might learn something, so was looking forward to it.

To which Winnie added thoughtfully, "Our world of spiritual life is really very small. We can always be broadened about the truth of everything. I'll be glad to learn what will be new to you." That was the beautiful part of their very close relationship; they were always able to share with each other.

While driving to Ken's who was one of the group, Joey thought upon how he had never read spiritual books of any kind except the Bible. He expected to hear a lot of new information which he thought would be very interesting. He found the street and watched address numbers shrink for a few blocks and soon found himself at Ken's address. He arrived just as George was arriving, and the two of them waited for the door to open. Ken greeted them warmly, and Joey was introduced to the others who were already there. Just then, Ken's wife came in asking how many wanted coffee. Joey was introduced to Helen, and he asked her if she studied with the group. She replied, "No, they talk way over my head. I can't understand what they're saying, so I don't try anymore."

Joey said, acknowledging, "I think I understand. Two years ago I didn't know anything about God, until I had my Light experience which changed my life." At that point all ears in the room were listening to Joey. "Maybe you'd like to hear my experience. It might help you understand?"

Ken nodded yes to Helen, and she said, "Okay, as soon as everyone gets their coffee. Maybe something will sink in." Everyone looked expectantly to Joey, and Joey knew he had to explain everything clearly to help Helen. This was turning out to be a little different than he had expected, so he thought he should tell the whole story about True Son."

When all were settled, he was given the floor. Joey told the whole story with all the emotions connected to it. None in the group had expected that. Then Joey told how he felt he needed to be spiritually educated in order to raise True properly, the resulting Light and love experience and what the Elders had said to him regarding what he was experiencing. Joey had looked at Helen most of the time while talking, because he felt she was the principle one in the room that needed to hear something more than the men had been studying. When he finished, he asked if everything he had said was clear. Helen asked, "Do you mean to say that the true nature of everyone is Light and love?"

Joey replied, "Yes. It may seem far from the self that we think ourselves to be, but in truth we are like our Creator--Great Spirit Who created us. You can see that by thinking of ourselves in this way, we would regard everyone to be much more than just a person who we perceive them to be. Our judgment of others would disappear, and we wouldn't go around judging anymore." Others in the room hadn't had a lesson quite as direct as that, and it made them think. Still looking at Helen he asked, "Does that help?"

Helen answered, "Yes, but I'll have to think about it. It's so huge." Joey nodded in agreement.

He looked around at the others wondering if there were any more questions. Apparently they were all digesting what he had said, when one asked, "What exactly do you mean by those you refer to as Elders?" Joey explained that they referred to themselves as friends from long ago, and that it later became clear to him that they were the Elders he had heard others mention on the reservation. Then Joey was asked, "Do they still speak to you?"

"Yes, they do, but not often." Joey replied. "A few months ago they told me about the new cycle of time we're now in, and how we're all going to know the truth of who and what we are, that we're the love and Light of Spirit, and how that is going to change our system of things to a beautiful humane way of living."

Several at once asked, "The New Age?"

Joey said, "Yes. I guess you could call it that. The Elders said that we're leaving the long age of separation behind us and are entering the new cycle of unification where everything will be bound together by love, and they said that we would find that love in our hearts, and through the love in our hearts, everyone would be equal."

One said, "I've never heard it put that clearly before. We've studied books that talked about the New Age, but I see it's a very simple, clear picture the Elders present. How do we find that love in our hearts?"

Joey said, "I've found truth to be always simple and clear. To find the love in our hearts, we only need to do two things: (1) We need to accept fully and completely that we are the love and Light expressions of our Creator. We need to practice thinking this until we really get to the place of knowing nothing different, and (2) We need to think happy, joyful thoughts all the time, which means that if we're not happy, we need to look at our thoughts that are not happy thoughts. In so doing we will find that those thoughts are not doing us any good, and they will fall away on their own. Happy thoughts are loving thoughts. Pure love is pure happiness, otherwise Jesus would not have taught that the kingdom of heaven is within us."

Another in the group spoke up and said, "We've been studying a long time trying to learn the truth of our being, and in a few words you have said clearly the truth we've been trying to learn. This is amazing!" Heads nodded in agreement.

George spoke and said, "Joey, I would appreciate hearing again what you said to me at the filling station about us all living in the heart of God?"

"Well, again, truth is very simple, but with our minds we try to make something big out of that which is so very simple, and that complicates things." Joey continued, "There being only the One Spirit, there can only be One Heart which is called the Heart of God. Because all of us are actually God, we all have the same One Heart that we call our own Heart, but it really is the Heart of God. There is no separation. When we experience the great love that is in our heart, we experience what some call the life of God. God or Great Spirit alone is all there is. We can be the One Spirit that is Light and love but we cannot possess it. We think we have ownership, but in truth, Spirit owns us, not in the way we think of ownership, because when we think of the vast intelligence of our Creator, we realize that we could never be in charge of our lives. God has always been in charge and will always be in charge. So we have a great need to let Spirit be in charge of our lives. I think we can all understand that. Do all of you agree?"

"So basically, "George said, "what you've just said is that we have no choice but to surrender to the Christ within ourselves?"

Joey replied, "If you try to surrender, you might find that you can't, because you're not ready to give everything up. You give in to Spirit at the moment, only to find later that your mind wants to take charge again. What I suggest is that you dwell on the greatness of Spirit, God, Christ or any other name that you prefer to call your Creator, until that greatness is so big, so wonderful, so intelligent that you give freely to it to run your life automatically all the time. Everyone has greatness within them that they have to discover, and when they do, they will know Who's in charge of their life. And they will know they are that greatness." Joey asked, "Does that help?"

George answered, "Yes, that's really clear. I can see how our thoughts actually lead us around by our noses. We don't really know a lot of things, but we try with our minds to think we do. I can see we have to be very honest with ourselves at all times in what we're thinking if we want to get on top of our thoughts. It seems to me that the mind can be very tricky at times and doesn't want to be discovered."

Joey said, "Now you're getting ahead of your mind and that's good, for as we catch our thoughts when we're thinking them, they subsequently get eliminated from our consciousness, and we begin to experience peace of mind. Doing this practice brings peace to the mind, which actually paves the way for the heart to open so we can experience the love that we are."

Another who had not spoken said, "You've put what we need to do right before us. Like Gandhi said, 'We must become the change we want to see in the world.' I see truth doesn't do us much good if we don't apply it to our lives. You've sure given us a good lesson tonight."

Heads nodded with murmurs of approval.

Joey said, "I've never studied like you have studied. In fact, I've never studied at all. This is my first time to be with a group that has studied spiritual information so earnestly, so I'm curious to know what you've come to understand--who've been your teachers, etc.? I feel like I need to know the truth that's being offered to the world."

Everyone was surprised. George offered, "To be honest, Joey, I don't mean to dismiss your honest intention, but all of us have deeply benefited by your sharing with us. We have never had such clear ideas of truth given to us in such simple words, and we really do thank you for it. I can understand what it is you want to know, but if we tried to load you up with what we've studied, I really feel we would load you up with a lot of information that wouldn't be as helpful to you as you would like. Instead, what I'd like to suggest, is make you a list of the most prominent spiritual books that I'm aware of and drop it off where you work. You would then have a chance to go over the list on your own and feel the ones that might interest you, and you could then contact me, and if we have them, we'd be happy to loan them to you." George looked at everyone and all agreed with the idea.

Joey answered, "I can see the honesty of your idea, and I thank you for your offer. It's a good idea. I'm guessing there are a lot of spiritual books out there, and to have a pared down list would save me a lot time and effort rather than having to try to find them on my own." There was small talk after that. They asked him where he lived and what he had been doing in the two years since he had his Light experience. That opened a whole new flood of information about speaking to all the reservations, and then he shared with them how he and Winnie had been given a truck and a new home.

They could hardly believe their ears. They really began to understand what a treasure they had in their midst that evening. They could see that he was God-chosen to do the work he was doing. They saw Joey's simplicity, and George asked if he could share Indian ways with them.

That took Joey by surprise, so he told them how his race had lived close to the land, respecting all life, and that when the Whites took the land from them and they were resigned to living on reservations, how that took their culture away from them which forced them to accept the ways of the White world. As a consequence they became a broken people. But, he told them, they had not lost interest in their heritage and were seeking to regain it. Joey used a lot more words in telling them about Indian ways, but that was the gist of how the Red Race was connected to the land.

They all saw that the way of Indian life was a mighty big subject, and to get to the point of really feeling Indian ways would take a lot of deeply devoted time and interest. George thanked Joey and said, "Once again you've surprised us with your knowing. I don't know where we could have gotten a better picture of your culture in such few words. Right now I feel very close to your people. Your people could no doubt teach us many things about living life in a deeper way than we in the White world know. So much of our lives seem to be just surface living. We're deeply immersed in materialism to the extent that we've lost a lot of feeling toward life."

Joey nodded that he understood and said, "The White way of education has blunted our feelings, which has robbed us of our innocence toward life and toward our Creator. Consequently, today there are many problems in our country that no one knows how to solve. And as we watch daily events unfold, it looks like we're going to have to learn the hard way. That's one of the big reasons why it's so vital to regain our true connection with our Creator, to know spiritually who and what we are in order to ride through these times and help others ride through the times ahead as well. This door of learning is open to everyone. All one has to do is choose it." Joey looked at the clock on the mantle, and said, "It's getting late, and we all have to work tomorrow, so it's best I get going. Thanks for letting me join you tonight. It's been very good. I've enjoyed meeting all of you." They all thanked him for coming and he left.

Here was a genuine person, they all thought. One said, "We should have given him something for his coming."

George said, "Well, let's all chip in and I can give it to him when I give him the list."

And so they did, grateful for the clarity that had greatly expanded their understanding. They didn't realize it, but their earnestness in desiring the truth had brought the truth to them in the form of Joey. In time as they would reflect on their evening, they would see the wonderful ways that Spirit works.

When Joey reached home, he told Winnie how the evening went, also saying that while driving home he realized how necessary it would be in the future to have copies of his little booklet to leave behind, because people just don't fully get the ideas he shared in one hearing. They really need something to refer to afterwards, because the ideas are so big and so new.

Winnie said knowingly, "I know you rock their boats with the big ideas you share. I rather imagine there are some young ones on the res who know something about computers who can help you."

Joey smiled, seeing the possibility that help was always close by.

CHAPTER 19

INDIAN MANIFESTO

J OEY WASTED NO TIME IN the next few days in starting to write. He knew what he wanted to say, but George had stopped by with the list of books and with their monetary gift. George made a point that the asterisked titles, were what he felt were the most important books. Joey noticed one right off, and said without thinking, "I think I would like to read *Autobiography of a Yogi*."

"Good, I have it. I'll drop it off tomorrow." George brought it the next day, and Joey started to read it that evening and was fascinated by it, so much so that he let writing the book rest for the time being. He had never read anything so captivating.

He saw that the author was a great Shaman. The book was so well written in personal experience that it drew him right into it.

Yogananda's life was a real eye opener. He tried to share it with Winnie, but all he did was make her curious, so she read it while he worked. Together their world of spiritual information expanded greatly, and it made them both wonder what else was going on in the world of truthful ideas that they knew nothing about.

They eventually would choose other books to read from George's list which would give them insightful expansions into truth presented in a number of different ways. In time, Joey would see that his feeling to know more about the truth that was being offered to the world proved to expand his own understanding, and he would find it comforting to know that truth was available to anyone who might be hungering for it. Both he and Winnie would in time feel that they had many spiritual allies in the world.

When Joey sat down to write, he read over what he had written and decided to start from scratch, because he couldn't get into his earlier mood. So he began again:

When one starts reading the many different tribal legends about the beginning of life on Earth from the Indian perspective, each has its pertinent value for each tribe. Each legend has to have a Creative Power to energize it, so while there are many legends about the beginning, there is only One Creator and one creation. The Creator is the Great Mystery of Great Spirit. Life is a great mystery for each of us, until Spirit reveals Itself to us as the Light and love that it is, not like light from the sun, but an inner Light that illumines all of creation, and not like the common love we have for each other, but a dynamic inner love that radiates from the heart that binds all things together as One. Spirit has created us as spiritual Beings of Light and love to forever be like Itself.

The Light of Spirit is the intelligence of God, and the Power and the Light of Spirit combined form the Love of Spirit, so Spirit

Love is also the Power and Light of Spirit. It is all One, even though our senses tend to tell us that everything is separate from everything else. There is no separation when we speak of Spirit; likewise there is no separation in our Creator's creation. It's this One Spirit that formed our ancestors' way of life. They lived in nature with nature, honored it and respected all life. This revered way of life has been lost, but we can regain it and know once again the beautiful Inner Life of Spirit.

To know and live consciously in Spirit, we have to reclaim our identity as Spirit. We may think we are something other than Great Spirit, but this is only our own way of believing ourselves to be something other than being the Great Spirit. Subsequently when we believe falsely, we live without the nourishment of the harmonious Inner Life, and life feels harsh in many ways and on many levels because of our low vibration of thought. We are minus the Light by which to see clearly, and we are minus the love that makes all life beautiful.

Since our true identity is Spirit, we must claim it by holding the thought all the time, "I am Spirit," in order to change from being a personal self to actually knowing we are Great Spirit. This, no doubt, will seem like a great leap for many, but when one reads the words of the Great White Shaman Jesus, He always pointed the way to the kingdom of His heavenly father that is within oneself, like, "You must be perfect, even as your heavenly father is perfect." "The kingdom of heaven is within you." "My kingdom is not of this world...my kingdom is now, not from hence."

Jesus was saying the kingdom of Light and love is within us, and that we must allow the perfection of that kingdom to be our life, that it is not off in time somewhere, but can be had every moment.

Regardless of how you have thought of yourself, you are the Light and love of Spirit, always have been and always will be. You could never be less, regardless of how you have thought of yourself. As Spirit is eternal Light and love, you are also eternal Light and love. You only need to reclaim your true identity. By thinking you are Light and love, you automatically raise your vibration to a higher rate. Your higher thought is conforming to the actuality of Spirit. By claiming your true spiritual identity, life becomes increasingly brighter, fuller and better. You see in new and fresher ways; optimism takes hold; the Allness of Spirit emerges into your feeling world, and you regain your connection with a greater, peaceful feeling of life.

A new life begins with thinking yourself to be as Great Spirit knows you to be. Great Spirit never made anything less than Itself, no matter what the life form might be, for each form has a part or a degree of Spirit consciousness in it. All life is Spirit life.

Think of a tree. It cannot grow aimlessly. Its branches grow into a beautiful symmetrical form by Spirit's direction, as does all of nature. Everything is part of the One Spirit life. Automatically, as you look upon a tree visually, you see the tree with your mind. You have taken the tree within yourself so that the tree has become a part of yourself. The tree is within you, as are all things. You cannot help but be a part of the One Spirit life. No one and nothing is left out.

When we contrast how all the created forms and the many intersecting energies combine to make life an integral wholeness, with the structured way that we in the human world try to make things work, we recognize that human ways fall far short of benefiting everyone. We see then that we have no alternative but to reclaim our true identity to live Spirit's way of life of love and Light.

Pure love, your true identity, radiates from your heart, the center of your Being which is not the physical heart that pumps blood throughout your body, but is the very core of your Being out of which flows your life-force. From this central core, you have access to all the wisdom of the Great Spirit. The heart's intelligence knows life as it is to be lived by you who are an extension of Itself. Our ancestors lived peaceably with all life, respecting their heart's intelligence, thus their lives were regulated by Spirit's wisdom easily and comfortably in all their ways by trusting Great Spirit to provide everything they needed.

As we practice saying, "I am Spirit," we steadily learn that Spirit reveals to us that It is really in charge of our lives, and that we can let go of the long-held idea that we are in charge when we consciously think that we are an identity other than Spirit. Our Creator never made two of us, Spirit and the little idea of our being something separate from Great Spirit. Our Creator extended Itself as us to be a point through which it could pour all its love, Light and intelligence for us to live life in all its perfect ways.

By saying, "I am Spirit," we get used to the idea that we are Spirit. We have nothing to lose and everything to gain when we see by the clarity of Spirit's Light and radiate life-giving love. We let go of a lot of tensions when we give control of our lives over to Spirit, which results in a mental relaxation of easiness unlike anything we've ever felt before.

This is the first part of **Indian Manifesto** which Spirit has given me to share in helping you to claim your true spiritual identity as love and Light.

The second and equally important part has to do with your thinking, which is really very simple. In order to live the beautiful Inner Life of Spirit, all your thoughts should be happy, joyful thoughts. All thoughts that do not make you feel happy need to be looked at in order that each thought be seen to see if it contributes harmoniously to creation. Happy, joyful thoughts come from your own spiritual intelligence that knows everything and everyone as part of Its spiritual creation. Thoughts of this nature are from your heart's love, and this kind of thinking can only make you happy. You are being the light and love that you are.

You may be thinking that happiness is a very small perspective to think from, but the Master Shaman said, "…narrow is the way which leadeth unto life, and few there be that find it." That was 2000 years ago, but the people of that time did not have the spiritual heritage that our ancestors have passed down to us, which today is known as the Good Red Path, the study of the Medicine Wheel or Sacred Hoop, the smoking of the Peace Pipe, Vision Quests, Sweat Lodges and Ceremonial Dances. Our knowing ancestors did not have all the modern things to clog their minds that we have to contend with today, which is why we need to look at all the thoughts we think, plus we have the need to look to see if we are harboring any poor feelings resulting from the White man taking our land. These kind of thoughts can destroy any well-being we might be enjoying.

The only world we live in is the world of our conscious making that is formed by our thoughts, and our thoughts determine solely how we feel. That we have been forced to live on reservations does not enslave us to live a reservation life. I have personally been lifted up much higher in my thinking as a result of my love and Light experience, to where now love and Light is my life.

Love and Light is our heritage, first from Spirit and secondly from our ancestors.

Perhaps reservation life, while felt to be mighty hard at times, can also be seen as a blessing, where we are not immersed in the White world of materialism. To be sure it encircles us, but we are not enslaved by it. I believe we are freer to reclaim our spiritual heritage on the reservation than if we were in the White world. We have a common denominator with each other which is a huge blessing. This does not make us any better than any other race, but we do have a heritage from our ancestors which others do not have. Our heritage tends to bind us together in love for one another. It's a huge plus in our lives.

So let our natural love for each other be like the wind to our backs to propel us into thinking what is good, true and beautiful in each other. Let all in the past be by-gones. If there is a need to forgive ourselves because of an ill we may be harboring toward another, then forgive when and where there is a need to forgive. We cannot live freely in Light and love when we continue to have ill feelings within ourselves. We are prisoners to bad feelings and infinitely free in good feelings.

Our feelings are always the one barometer we can trust for accuracy. Our feelings do not lie. Feelings easily tell us the big difference between feeling happy and feeling unhappy. The truth is our thoughts mean everything to us. We regain our ancestral heritage by thinking happy thoughts.

This is a good place to repeat what the Elders have said regarding the new cycle of time we have entered. **"What you are seeing in your world is the birthing of a new day, a new time in our Creator's Great Cycle of Times. Your humanity, as a whole, is leaving the long age of separation and is entering** *a new time of unification where everyone will know the ways of their Creator. All people will become unified by the agent of love in their hearts. They will come to know that their nature is love like their Creator is love. Thus for each one, their own love will lead the way, and love will bind all together as One in equality, in worth and in intelligence, out of which even the history of separation will not be remembered."*

From the Elders' words we can see that we are in a transition period between an old outgoing age of immense human suffering and struggles and entering a new age in our Creator's Great Plan where only unity of purpose on every level is foreordained, which is all the more reason to become thoughtful of our true identity to regain the simplicity of thought that our ancestors knew so well.

Nobody has to tell us that humanity's old structured ways of doing business are no longer working. At every turn, a new difficulty emerges that demands a solution that will satisfy everyone. It is saddening to witness a civilization of people that doesn't know how to cooperate with each other when facing dilemmas and problems. The problem of not knowing how to cooperate is, in my opinion, a people problem that will not go away until people know their true spiritual identity. So when we look out upon the world and are witness to its many struggles, let us not be engulfed by them. As we must claim our own true spiritual identity, we also know that all others must claim their own true identity. The problems we see can only be solved spiritually. This is the time we are in. Old ways that do not benefit everyone must give way to spiritual ways. This, as long promised, is the transition period between the old and the new. A new Cycle of Time has begun.

While we of our Red Race have to contend with what has happened to us in the past, we also have to contend with these difficult times. Our solution for any contentions that seemingly face us is to claim our true spiritual identity and to think only happy thoughts.

In so doing, we gain that highly cherished state of being free from thinking thoughts to where we live in an awareness of Great Spirit's stillness. The freedom attained from no longer needing to think all those extra thoughts that we think daily is an immeasurable accomplishment.

Seldom, if at all, is any thought given to this highly precious state. People long for peace in the outer world, little realizing that it is really inner peace they long for. Unless one is seeking spiritual truth, the many clamoring voices that claim they have answers to the problems in the outer world hardly ever mention the highly desired state of having inner peace of mind. Thus, individually, we are left to learn that inner peace is our solution in how to live in these difficult times.

When we detect that we are thinking unhappy thoughts, our detection gives us the chance to either eliminate that type of thought from our thinking or replace that thought with a happy or true spiritual thought. This is the road to attain peace of mind, that treasured state of being free of thinking thoughts which allows us to be in the awareness of Spirit.

When we look at all our thoughts truthfully, the past is no longer with us and the future hasn't come yet, which leaves us living in the current Now moment, the only place anyone can fully live. Great Spirit acts only in the current moment, so it is useless to try to live in past moments or past times, and it is equally folly to fear the future or think hopefully that the future *somehow will be better than the present. These are thoughts outside of the Now moment.*

Being present in the Now moment is the only place to live. In the peace of the Now moment that is without thought of any kind, is when Spirit is able to come into our experience, whether it's the peace of God, the love of God or the Light of Spirit awakening us. There isn't any other time in all existence except the Now moment.

When we are listening to our thoughts, we will discover just how many of our thoughts are either in the past or in the future. So many of our thoughts are memory, many of which have to do with people. It is surprising how many extraneous thoughts we think daily, for unknowingly all our extra thoughts have surrounded our heart and have prevented love and light from being lived. It is what we have stored in our subconscious mind which surrounds our heart that each of has to deal with, because we alone have put those thoughts there.

All the ideas of being separate from Spirit and from each other have the need of being eliminated. Likewise everything in our subconscious that has no connection to Great Spirit also has to be eliminated. When we reduce our thinking to thinking only happy thoughts, that effort brings the treasured peace of mind to everyone. All of us have our own subconscious thoughts to work on, and what starts out to be what seems to be a huge effort does diminish in size quickly, as we feel the peaceful benefits that result from our efforts.

Regardless of how each of us may view our self, we, in the main, are a free people. Our true identity cannot be withheld from us. Great Spirit commissions each one of us to be Its spiritual messenger of love and Light in this world. The beauty and *simplicity of the **Indian Manifesto** is that it is open to all wherever one might be. The new Cycle of Time that beckons all to get on board, is a wonderful time in which to be living.*

Joseph Long-Seeing

Joey found the words came quite easily, but he pored over what he had written many times before he felt satisfied. Then he gave it to Winnie to read, hoping she would be able to add something to it. She read it through once and thought he had said all that could be said in both parts of the booklet. She thought it would serve the purpose it is meant to serve. Joey had kept it simple and thorough. She could see that the readers would be able to easily identify with their own state of mind as they read the booklet. Then she gleaned through it two more times for errors. Finding a few she marked in red she gave it back congratulating him on writing a very clear, helpful teaching reminder.

They agreed that 100 copies would be enough to start with. Joey asked around for the cheapest way to have it printed. When he asked George about it and let him read it, George said that it would be good for his group to study, and also offered, "I believe those on the reservations will find this very useful too," and then said, "I think our study group can have your 100 copies printed for you." Joey thanked him profusely; what a wonderful outworking. It sent good feelings soaring.

Joey composed a cover letter, saying that he felt impressed to write the little booklet and hoped that it would be helpful. If they needed more copies, he could supply them with the needed number for a little donation to cover the costs. He and Winnie were to be greatly surprised at the numerous requests for the large number of copies they would get, which kept them quite busy. Most of all, Joey was happy that the booklet turned out to be useful. He remembered well that he had no one to talk to about his early experiences. Even though he had Winnie to share with, he had no real instruction, which made him feel that instructions would be very helpful. The booklet was a helpful way for people to share and discuss spiritual ideas. He knew that the shared perspectives of others often produced an understanding that one couldn't get alone. He was grateful.

Chapter 20

True's Growing Years

THE NEXT THREE YEARS WENT by quickly. Joey spoke here and there periodically, mostly to White gatherings. Occasionally he had been invited to speak at some liberal Christian churches, each time that he spoke proved to be a new experience, as he let Spirit use him to speak the right words for each group to hear. Joey was surprised each time how receptive the congregants were to his message. He always took a good supply of booklets with him which he knew would be helpful for them to retain his message. He was to later find that the understanding he had gained at the churches would be useful in guiding True in his own spiritual work that lay before him.

True wasn't really aware how extra observant his parents were as they watched him. He just felt that to be natural as he had nothing else in which to relate their deep interest in him. Winnie and Joey came to know from watching True closely, that he definitely was born with inner sight or vision. Both of them had often seen True seeing something or someone they could not see. Many times they would watch True look up from what he was doing to look at something and laugh.

Then, one day when they were all outside, True looked away from what he was doing to see that he was possibly seeing someone in the unseen, because they could hear True speaking an answer to someone. So Joey asked True, "Who were you speaking to?"

True answered, "A friend."

"How do you know your friend? Does your friend have a name?" Joey asked.

"Yeah," True replied. "He's a friend from long ago. His name is Sunbird. He makes me laugh when he tells what we did long ago."

"Do you remember from long ago?" How long ago?"

"Yeah; what he tells me makes me remember a trick we played on a friend. We had lots of fun then. I just remember it was long ago."

"Do you remember your name?" asked his father.

"People called me Strong," True said. "I remember I liked being called Strong. It always made me feel good."

Joey and Winnie were amazed. They had never known anyone who could remember a past life, and to remember so clearly, nor had they ever had any conversation on the subject, so this was brand new to them. It opened a whole new vista of expanded understanding. They both pondered deeply what True had said, and after he had gone to sleep that night, they both came to the conclusion that no one, not even their mothers were to know about True remembering his past life. The Elders had said that True should be supported in every way. They learned more than ever that True was definitely not an average child.

From then on, they both watched True more closely. Both noted that many times he seemed to be looking past a person rather than look directly at the person, which made them wonder what he was seeing. One day when Winnie was shopping and noted True's eyes following a person for some time, and wondering she asked True, "What's so special about the woman you're looking at?"

True nonchalantly said, "She has the prettiest coloring around her?"

"What do you mean by coloring? How do you see coloring-- where do you see coloring?"

True said, "Can't you see it? It's all around her body--pretty pink with some light blue. It's very pretty. It's something like your coloring, Mommy."

That response took Winnie completely by surprise. At the same time she thought she should have known better. She knew he had inner vision which let him see far more than just external things. She had just never given thought to True's ability to see auras, which to him must be a big part of what he sees naturally. She hadn't ever seen an aura around anyone, so it just wasn't a part of her life. She shared with Joey what had happened that afternoon, and both agreed they had to keep silent about True's ability to see auras too. There just was no point for others to look upon True as unusual. His so-called natural recognition being True Son was enough for him to have to handle. Around the res and in assemblies True was always given respect, but not in a special way, which Winnie and Joey greatly respected in return.

Naturally they talked about True's schooling. They had gone to school on the reservation and felt it all right to send True there. There would be his own kind that he was used to, and if need be, they could talk with his teachers if they had to, knowing there is a change of teachers from time to time. They would see.

There hadn't been any children of True's age in his neighborhood to play with, so school was going to be a whole new world to him. True was no different than most children when they see someone their own age in a store or in the mall. He stared at them and at times was friendly, so his parents felt he would get along all right. They had talked with him for several months about starting school, so True was eager and could hardly wait for the summer months to go by so he could go to school. School was all he talked about. They felt his eagerness was a good precedent to his liking school.

It turned out that the new kindergarten teacher was a replacement for the previous one who had just had a baby. When the new teacher went around the room and everybody had to say their name, she was somewhat surprised when True said his name was True Son. She didn't want to question him in front of the others, so she asked other teachers about him. They didn't live on the res so they didn't know distinctly. They gave her vague information about what they had heard, which whet her curiosity all the more, so she decided she would have to visit True's parents to learn the full story. She felt it important that she know about all the children in her class.

True came home all excited about school, telling them all about it. It was a fun day for him, how many new kids he met and what a nice teacher Miss Julie was. When Winnie got the surprising call from his teacher that she wanted to meet with her, she couldn't figure out why. All the teacher said was that she needed to know more about True Son. Little did Winnie know they would become fast friends. When she asked if Winnie could come to school tomorrow afternoon at 3:00, Winnie replied that she could.

When she told Joey about the unusual call from True's teacher, Joey's ability to long-see kicked in, and he assured her that everything was going properly and that there was nothing to be worried about, saying, "You'll like her."

Winnie dropped True off at her mother's and arrived at school with Miss Julie waiting for her. They exchanged greetings with Julie saying that she had never taught on a reservation before and that True Son's name intrigued her, and that she also noted that Winnie's name was Jennifer WindSong and that her husband's name was Joseph Long-Seeing. She explained that their names must mean something and that if she knew their meanings, she would be more in tune with them and it would help her understand True in a fuller way.

Winnie thought that to be very logical, so she began to tell Julie all about herself and Joey, their name meanings, and all the detail rolled right out of her, the stillbirth of their child, the eagle sighting, and finding True on the entry to the church, Joey's light experience and his subsequent sharing of his experience with all the reservations. Julie was visibly moved. Kids were special in her life, but she had never heard of anything like this. Julie had a soft heart which absorbed Winnie's sharing like a sponge. She somehow felt deeply connected to Winnie and couldn't really explain it. Winnie's history really resonated with her. And Winnie also felt a closeness with Julie which was almost sister-like, although she never had a sister. Each felt a simultaneous trust in each other. A beautiful connection was made in an hour's time. Each felt meeting each other was extraordinary. Hugging, they said goodbye to each other and would keep in touch.

Early the next week Winnie was surprised when she answered the phone in the evening to hear Julie's voice. Julie said that she had been thinking of Winnie all week-end and was wondering if they could get together and have dessert somewhere after dinner tomorrow.

"Wonderful--yes," was out of Winnie's mouth before she knew it.

Julie said, "Fine. I'll pick you up at 7:30. Okay?" She got directions from Winnie and was at Winnie's at 7:30 the next evening. This was going to be a new event for Winnie, as she had no one really close on the res except Joey and her mother. Their time flew by quickly in conversing and sharing their lives and their feelings with each other. They got to know each other quite well in a short time.

It was about 9:15 when Julie pulled into Winnie's. Winnie said, "Can you come in for a few minutes to meet Joey?" From all that Winnie had told Julie about Joey, she felt like she already knew him. So she said, "Sure."

There was happiness and some laughing in meeting Joey. True hadn't gone to sleep yet, because he wasn't used to his mother not being there and hearing extra noise in the house was something he wasn't used to either. Being curious he came out of his room to be really surprised to see Miss Julie. There was kidding and laughing and Joey thinking that True should be getting back to bed, said to him, "Com'n little Buddy, it's kind of past your bedtime; let's go back to bed, and I'll see that you're covered and turn out the light."

True didn't need much coaxing, so when he was getting in bed he said, "Miss Julie is Singing Water and Mommy is Singing Flower."

Joey looked at his son and wondered, what's he talking about? So he asked, "What do you mean Miss Julie is Singing Water and Mommy is Singing Flower?"

"That's what they were called long ago."

Joey thought, oh, oh and asked, "How do you know, True?"

True said, "It's just there; you can see it."

Joey thought to ask, "What do you see, True?"

True, a little perturbed at what seemed to him to be foolish questions, said, "Well, they're sisters and they look a lot like each other."

Joey thought and said, "You mean they're twins? You've seen twins before. Do they look like they're twins?" True shook his head yes and crawled under his blanket.

Joey thought it best not to go any further, kissed True on the forehead, and said, "Sleep tight" and turned out the light. Joey thought he had better talk to Winnie alone about this. At the moment he felt it was not for anyone else to hear.

When Joey joined the two of them again, Julie said, "True's really a fine boy. It shows that you've taught him well. It's a pleasure to have him in my class."

Joey said, "Thank you. We've wondered how we've been doing. It's really nice to see that he's getting a good start in school. That means a lot to us."

Julie acknowledged Joey's feelings and said, "I'd better be going. Thanks, Winnie, for taking the time to share with me. I've really enjoyed being with you."

Winnie echoed, "Ditto. It's been really nice. Maybe you would join us for supper some time?"

Julie replied that she'd love to as she hugged Winnie goodbye. Turning to Joey she said, "I'm really glad I got the chance to meet you, Joey. It's always good to be able to put a face with a name." Joey nodded in approval. Saying good night, she left.

Joey said, "She's a nice lady. I'm glad you two hit it off."

To which Winnie said, "I really enjoy her company."

Joey thought he'd have a little fun, so he said, "Do you know why you two hit it off so nicely?"

Winnie murmured, "No."

Joey smiling said, "You were twins in a past life."

"You don't really know that, Joey. You shouldn't say something you don't mean."

Joey said, "It's true. Your name was Singing Flower and Julie's name was Singing Water."

Winnie wasn't enjoying Joey's kidding and said, "Com"n now. Stop fooling around."

Joey said, "I'm having fun with you, but it's all true. True told me all this while getting back in bed."

Winnie's features took on a wondering look. This was really surprising and would take some digesting. "Do you mean to tell me that True could see into a past life that Julie and I were twin sisters?"

"That's what True saw. He said, 'I just see it.'" And then Joey filled her in how he didn't feel he should press True too much. He wanted to keep it like a natural conversation.

They were both in deep wonder. True could see into past lives? This was a lot more than just having an inner vision of being able to see in other dimensions. They both concurred with each other that this was not a quality that could be taken as lightly as a means for others to want to know that True could tell them how to solve their personal problems. This was a quality that would be useful in helping others to see truth more clearly.

They both wondered if they should tell Julie. They agreed that it might be too much for her to absorb right now. They would have to wait to see what depth her friendship with Julie would take. Then again, it might all unfold naturally. They thought that since Julie had a Native American life as an Indian, remembrances might bleed through. They would let the future take care of itself. It wasn't as easy for Winnie as it was for Joey, for Winnie had good feelings she wanted to share with Julie, but wisdom came first.

Actually, the way it turned out was that True at times would call Miss Julie by her Singing Water name. When this happened several times, Julie began to wonder why he addressed her by that name. Rather than question him, Julie asked Winnie about the Singing Water idea that True had about her. The door opened naturally for Winnie to share the whole story. Julie was not really too surprised.

Part of deciding to teach on the reservation was because of her interest in Native American life. Julie and Winnie's friendship kept growing deeper and deeper, enriching both of their lives. Love was binding them together once again. It was proving that love is forever, although neither of them saw it on that philosophical level.

During that kindergarten year True at times said odd things to some of the kids, and in return he got bewildering looks. Slowly True began to realize that the things that he saw so naturally, the other kids couldn't see at all. So he learned early on that he should keep to himself what others could not see. He learned wisdom fairly early that he was different in that respect from the other kids, and by not revealing what he was seeing; it helped him to be like an ordinary kid fitting in with the rest.

By the time True became seven, he started to question everything about life. More happenings in life were getting his attention, and it was puzzling to him why people were so mean to each other. He often talked with his parents about the problems he saw people having. At that early age, Joey found it difficult to put truth into simple words that True could understand, but True was so sincere in wanting to understand, that he more or less forced Joey to make it clear until he understood. Joey marveled that he had interest in such deep things at his young age. By the time True was ten, he was wise way beyond his years. Yet he ran and played with other kids and liked playing baseball. He often found himself in the midst of squabbles and could offer ideas that were acceptable to smooth things out between kids. He grew up normally in all the natural ways.

When he entered the tenth grade, his teachers started promoting the idea of going to a college or university upon graduating from high school. He talked to his parents about it and the real relevance it had to do with the Spirit life he knew himself to be. Neither his mother nor his dad had gone to college, and he thought they had attained so much that he couldn't see the usefulness of getting a degree. He would continue learning what school was teaching him and would keep an open mind. Maybe there was something he should learn that would be helpful later on. He had learned early on that the Truth that he knew himself to be, was living its life through him, and he was content to follow Truth's direction. Thus he looked at formal education in the manner of what allowed him to be in deeper attunement with his spiritual Self. When formal education seemed to obscure his own Truth, he really questioned the validity of that teaching. He had found earlier that it did not pay to counter what was being taught. All it did was cause an upset in the class, because what he had to offer had no relevance to the subject. That did no good whatsoever. So he learned to go along with what the teaching was, but he didn't have to believe it. He thought to himself numerous times, that some schooling was teaching ignorance and not the truth. Life seemed to be all about everyone trying to make a living off of each other. There was an ethics of fairness underlying what was being taught, but no mention of the Truth that everyone is really love. It wasn't easy for him to watch his fellow students being programmed to believe in false ideas, but luckily he knew the truth of who everyone really was, and that grounded him to keep silent.

What he was learning in his last two years of high school, taught him that college was going to be a deepening of that same false teaching about how to live, and that was something he didn't want to participate in. He felt that if there was any subject he needed to know more about, he could study on his own to learn what he needed to learn when he needed to learn it. He could clearly see that his life was about waking people up from their hypnotized slumber and not about accumulating a wealth of things. So all through high school he remained totally aware of being the Truth he knew himself to be. In spite of being kind of an oddball in school, he was extremely bright, and his always happy state of mind magnetically drew kids to him.

While he didn't graduate with scholarly honors, he was highly respected and was elected president of his class, which he took in stride. When he spoke at his graduation, he never made up a speech. He just spoke from his heart, telling how great his teachers were and how many wonderful friends he had in his class. He thanked his teachers for making his high school years a great learning experience, and he thanked his fellow students for all the good times they had together. It was a simple speech he gave, but it touched the heart of everyone, especially his parents. True had been true to the Truth he knew himself to be.

Chapter 21

True Introduces Himself to the World

ONE PERSON WHO HAD BEEN to True's graduation whom nobody seemed to notice because of the excitement of the graduates getting their diplomas, was Ron. Ron was a fixture on the res and was in his late fifties. When he listened to True speak, something of the Spirit spoke to him; something resonated within him. He couldn't define it, but he felt that True had something to offer people at his Sunday morning service. He let a couple of weeks roll by before contacting True. When he talked to True about his strong feelings, True was very surprised. He hadn't been to Ron's church, so he said to Ron that he was very green at speaking at a church service. Ron's answer was quite persuading. "I know what you mean. There's always the first time for everyone, but you live the Truth that you are, and that message will come out from you naturally. I know it; I can feel it. I heard you speak at your graduation, and I know what I felt."

True couldn't deny Ron's deep sincerity and said, "Maybe I should give it a try. I'll let the Truth within me say what it wants to say."

Ron's face brightened into joy. "I'm so glad to hear you say that! People need waking up, and I know they'll respond to your freshness of truth." Ron gave True all the details.

True told his parents about his meeting with Ron, and down deep they both smiled a knowing smile. True was beginning his destined spiritual work at about 18 years of age. Both knew the world needed True's caliber of consciousness. They often had heard the Spirit of True speak so naturally about the order of things in life that it had made them blink at the purity of what they heard. Many times later after True had moved out, they realized what a great spiritual resource True was--if only they had known what questions to ask, they could have gained much knowledge about the universal order of things.

When the scheduled Sunday morning came, the church was packed, including standing room only. Ron had put the word out that True was going to speak. At long last everyone was going to hear for the first time from the one whom they had longed to hear. True was surprised at the packed church. His parents thought the church would be filled, but not to the extent of there being no standing room left. It was hard to put into words what they were feeling in total, but gratitude was probably what they were feeling the most.

Right after the opening of the service, Ron said, "I know we're all ears to hear True this morning, so we're going to dispense with our regular order of service to give True all the time he needs. Maybe we'll have time for a few questions." Then he gave the lectern over to True saying that he really needed no introduction.

True was a little nervous, and he said so. Then he said, smiling, "I'm really happy so many of you are here. I'd better not disappoint you." There was a little chuckle that ran through church.

Continuing, he said, "I find it unusual that you want to hear from one so young. I'm sure my dad would be able to share more of his gained wisdom than I can. But then there really is no age to Spirit. Spirit speaks many times through little ones if we listen closely to them. They often try to tell us things, but our ears aren't really tuned to what they have to say. They speak of simple things, so that's what I want to share with you, the simple things of life, your life, what concerns you the most. Do you know that your Spirit, the Truth of whom you are, is always closer to you than your next breath? Do you really know that? Do you think about the Truth that you are every moment of your day, day in and day out?

"Well, if you don't, you are really missing out on the biggest part of your day, because the world can't give you what is your true nature. The world can only give you things that have their fleeting moments, but your Spirit gives you Life with a capital L. And Spirit's Life is full of everything you could ever ask for--love, light, peace, harmony, well-being--and it's all right within you all the time just waiting for you to let it come forth from inside yourself. The outer world can't compete with that.

"I'm not giving you anything new. My dad wrote a little booklet many years ago that contained the wisdom of the ages. In it he said you only needed to do two things: (1) Claim your spiritual Self, and (2 Think only happy thoughts. That is so simple. You see, my friends, you must come to love the Spirit that you are as much as Spirit, your Greater Self, loves you. Spirit is love, and life only gets better when we love each other as much as we love ourselves.

"Now, the real problem is that we love our personal self more than we love our Spirit Self, the Truth of our Being. When we love our personal self, we have the wrong kind of love which is directed inward toward ourselves, whereas when we love our Spirit Self, our love flows outward toward others, and this makes life very, very beautiful. Don't you agree?"

He saw a lot heads nod yes. Continuing he said, "You see, I know you know this, but in the busyness of life, these two ideas get put on your back burner. The outer world is a big robber of your attention and of your time, and I know life can be very difficult for some of you here on the res, but it's difficult out in the White world too. They have to deal with a whole world of distractions, but that's life in this third dimensional Earth world. No matter how great our intentions might be before our birth into this world, this world is a mesmerizing place.

"This is what we need to become aware of. We need to know that we are already Truth. We need to know that we are the Spirit that gives life to our bodies and the energy that enables us to think our thoughts.

"Spirit is who you are. This is a spiritual world. Our ancestors knew that. They knew everything had a life and a purpose. Everyone on this planet is here to know they are Spirit and that each has a deep spiritual purpose, but this planet's vibration gets their attention, and they become lost in the lower, slower vibration which automatically reduces their awareness to being something other than the Great Spirit that they are. Consequently their feeling world diminishes from feeling absolutely great to actually feeling just about nothing. That is the way with this world. It robs you of your beautiful spiritual feelings, and then you have to get some satisfaction from feeling the things of this third dimensional world.

"Don't get me wrong. This is a beautiful world in every aspect, but I can tell you that your spiritual world exceeds this world by far. It's only from knowing your spiritual world that you get to see the true picture of this world. You see, my friends, everything must be seen from its true spiritual perspective, otherwise we try to live blindly, by that I mean we try to live by guessing what things are for, and we often guess wrongly and then have to pay in difficulties and in hardships. By going to our spiritual identity in thought and staying there, we leave our travails behind us.

"When we live from our true spiritual perspective, light opens our eyes to see clearly and love flows freely from our hearts. None of us can be other than the Light and love that we are. We may try to be something else for a time, but we can never be less than the One Creator that created us. Our Light and love may become diminished for a time, but that Light and love can never fully disappear. We have a longing, a thirst for something that can lift us out of the drabness of our feeling world, but we don't know what it is that we're longing for. That's why we have to search our own hearts to see what it is that we're lacking. This outer world cannot satisfy what we're lacking. It can give us momentary pleasures, but that soon fades; it does not last. We can be grateful for the blessings that we have in this world, but that does not satisfy us completely.

"That's why we have to search our hearts; we have to plumb the depths within ourselves to honestly know what we're lacking. If we do this looking within, we will see how barren we are inside without the warm, assuring Presence of Spirit that we can feel. The Spirit of you is the Truth with a capital T. You can't find the Truth of who and what you are unless you find it within yourself. And when you find it, you will find that it will never let you go, because Spirit has found Spirit, and out of this finding, you will find everything. You will have found that you are Home, because you will know that your Heart contains all the riches of your feeling world that make up the splendor of your Inner Life. There simply is no comparison between the Inner Life of Spirit and the outer life of this world.

"Man tries to regulate the outer world and is failing in every way, because he is not letting Spirit be his Inner Life. Man is the supreme life form on the earth, and all of nature will respond harmoniously when he lets his Inner Life be the activity in the outer world.

"Let us see clearly that without the knowing of the Inner Life of Light and love, we will never enjoy the full measure of living life in this world as it was meant to be. It's like baking a pie without all the tasty ingredients, all you have is the crust. That's not even a pie.

"Liken the pie to the times we're in. All the ingredients are the complicated technologies that are supposed to make a beautiful pie. We only have to ask ourselves, can everybody eat this pie? Mankind is slipping away into a vast technological mixture that is really starting to control him, because he finds it so necessary to keep up with the technological advances. It is much like the economy which is so out of hand because of its lack of built-in wisdom that it is now like the tail wagging the dog in trying to keep itself afloat. Likewise, technology will be seen to be too big for everyone's britches. It has its own built in weaknesses. Like the economy which has no wisdom to make it sustainable, so does technology lack wisdom in its overall purpose.

"Therefore the workings of the outer world are fogging everybody's mind. The outer world appears to be everything, but people are beginning to see that it is not everything, that there has to be a greater meaning to life, and many are questioning what that meaning is.

"I bring the outer world to your attention because we have to live in it, but how to live in it comfortably is the question. That question has already been answered. You are Spirit, find and experience the Spirit within yourself, and you will have the proof that you have the answer to the meaning of life. Remember, Spirit is all there is, likewise you can only be the love and Light of Spirit. You might think of yourself as a little self, but Spirit did not make you as a little self. Your Creator created you like Itself. This simply cannot be denied forever, as some are wont to do. But, in time, all will find their way home to the Spirit that they are. That is the destiny that our Creator has baked into Its Great Plan. We here have our destiny before us. All we have to do is move into synchronicity with our destiny. It's that simple."

Looking at the clock, True asked Ron if there was any time left for questions, and Ron nodded yes. So True asked if any one had a question. After a few moments, a hand went up, asking, "Are there any books that we can read that will help us to find the Truth within ourselves?"

True replied, "I don't want you to think I'm not answering your question, but you are your own best possible book to read. There are many books out there that are helpful to many, but again, you are your most helpful book to read. By looking within yourself, you will discover the things that you are holding onto that prevent you from going deeper within yourself. Eliminate those things; they are hurtful to you. You will find that you don't want to hang onto those hurtful things, and they will disappear from the world within yourself.

"This friend has asked a question that pertains to everyone. Everyone has to look at their own self-created stuff, so to speak. How else will you know what needs to be gotten rid of? Thank you for asking that very important question. Who else has a question?"

Another hand went up, asking, "How will we know which are hurtful things?"

"By your feelings. Your feelings will tell you how you feel about something or someone. Remember, you are to have only happy thoughts. You will know what makes you happy or unhappy. Your personal thoughts are your life, and they mean everything to you. It just might be that you have some unhappy thoughts within yourself. Looking at your thoughts is a very simple process. You're looking to see what it is that is not happy within yourself." As politely as he could, True asked, "Do you understand?" There was a nod yes. "Does anyone else have a question?"

Another hand went up, saying, "The world appears to be in turmoil. What do you see in the long run of things? How do you see it all ending?"

True answered, "That's a sixty four thousand dollar question to which we would all like to see the answer. What we need to understand is that if we keep our attention on the unsolvable problems that keep rising, we will be consumed by their seeming detrimental nature. The only reason that we keep our attention on them is to see how they might work out for the good of all. We need to remember that the problem we may be looking at has no viable solution that benefits all, because there is no love present in it, therefore it cannot have a happy, beneficial solution. In time our Creator's plan is for a new age which will allow everyone to live spiritually together as One. Everything that happens between now and then is really none of our business. Our business is to become the expression of the new age. I don't know if this is the answer you wanted to hear, but that's how Spirit has shown me that the new age will come about. The new age that is to be is about finding our individual place in it as a spiritual being enjoying the spiritual life. The rest will all pass away. That's about as clear as I can make it. Okay?" Again there was a nodding of yes. "I see Ron motioning to me. I think we've run out of time. It's been fun. Thanks for coming." With that Ron took over thanking True through the applause. And offering prayers, he took up the Sunday offering.

People were not too quick to leave their pews. The spiritual impact of True's words had been deeply felt. True enjoyed shaking hands with each one as they left. An energy of Oneness had permeated the air. And, of course, Ron was really grateful that his friends had heard the truth about themselves, just as he had envisioned True capable of delivering. He thought it was just the spiritual jolt that was needed. He remembered the spiritual jolt Joey had given at that memorable potluck 17 years previous. Ron was really full of joy and gratitude as he handed True the whole of the Offering. Ron didn't know it, but getting True to speak had a double-barrel purpose. News of True's speaking got around the reservations fast, and it wasn't long before they wanted True to speak to them also. True's work had begun.

Joey and Winnie took True to dinner during which they told True they thought he had been very effective with the words that had poured out of him. They said they both felt the energy in the church change from kind of a wide mixture of anxious expectations to a cohesive feeling of attentiveness. They congratulated True on letting a strong, acceptable spiritual message reach eager ears. They, too, were surprised at how the church was packed, and Joey said, "Don't be surprised if word gets around that you've started to speak. Joey's long-seeing had opened his vision saying, "You're going to be very busy speaking around. You're going to grow much stronger within yourself very fast."

True replied, "I think I see what you're seeing. Yes, it's going to be an interesting ride, both on the reservations and off." He was seeing, as his life stretched out before him, through being in his own spiritual Presence, the great unfolding of his life as a speaker and as a physical healer. Being White-skinned, he saw himself moving as freely in the White world as in Native American locations all across the country. And in this picture of his future, he also saw the one who would join him as his spiritual partner, but she would not be in the physical. His mental focus was broken by his reaction. He thought that was definitely going to be a very interesting development in a way in which he had never dreamed, even though he knew there was an energy exchange going on all the time between the two dimensions.

When True shared with his parents what he had just envisioned, that perked both of them to wonder about his destined future. He would be a physical healer too? And he would have a spiritual partner, but she wouldn't be physically in this world with him? That was far beyond anything they had ever envisioned. True was a True Son of Great Spirit. Now his parents saw that he was going to introduce a new dimension of spiritual Reality to an awakening world. Joey's long-seeing ability allowed him to see the barriers between the dimensions of earth life and the so-called after-life dissolve to become the Wholeness of the One Life of Great Spirit. True's spiritual life was to be a great unveiling message to the world.

To be continued

About the Author

Don Knight is a retired Unity minister. In early September of 2009, His Higher Consciousness gave him the new spiritual name Seven Arrows to replace or add to the previous Spirit given name of Uno, meaning One as the ONE that is all.

Seven Arrows is more one's own personal Medicine Wheel than it is a personal name. The first four arrows represent the Four Directions of the Medicine Wheel or Sacred Hoop, the teaching that one is the wholeness of everything. From the North we learn the beautiful words that form the ancient spiritual wisdom. These beautiful words are empty of feeling, until we turn to the South where we experience the innocence and warmth of Love that gives life and meaning to the wisdom from the North. When we face the diversities of life from the West, we are obliged to look within ourselves introspectively, to peer into every dark corner of our consciousness to eliminate all that is hiding in the darkness, so that when facing the illuminating Light from the East, every area within becomes flooded with Its all-enfolding brilliance. The fifth arrow represents Mother Earth, the All-Provider of everything in our life. Deeper revelation of the fifth arrow reveals that when we walk upon our Earth Mother, we actually walk upon our own Self. The sixth arrow represents Grandfather Sun, Father Sky, Sister Moon, all the planets and all the heavenly bodies in the Cosmos with which we have daily exchanges of energy. The seventh arrow represents the Great Mystery, the Great Spirit Creator of everything. So Seven Arrows is the Sacred Hoop, or Medicine Wheel that encompasses and contains all the positive, animal, plant and mineral Totem meanings that promote the opening of the Heart's spiritual life.

Seven Arrows is really everyone's name, as it represents the application of living the Medicine Wheel that forms a large portion of the Indian Good Red Path which empowers everyone to know they are Great Spirit.

The Author has written the following books:

"BEING - Guidelines to the Heart"

"Return to Wholeness"

"Perception - Journey into Universal Love"

"Perfection - Living the New Age Life"

"Creative Sharing - The New Economy"

"SON of GOD Sayings - Let the Good Times Roll"

"TRUE SON"

Email: sevenarrowsdjk@gmail.com

www.Heartlightways.com